Lemon Drop Falls

Lemon Drop Falls

Heather Clark

JOLLY
FiSH
PRESS

Mendota Heights, Minnesota

First Edition
First Printing, 2022

Book design by Jake Slavik
Cover design by Jake Slavik
Cover illustration by dirclumsy (Beehive Illustration)
Font attribution: GelPens by Shara Weber

Jolly Fish Press, an imprint of North Star Editions, Inc.

This is a work of fiction. Names, characters, places, and incidents are either the product of the author's imagination or are used fictitiously, and any resemblance to actual persons living or dead, business establishments, events, or locales is entirely coincidental.

Library of Congress Cataloging-in-Publication Data (pending)
978-1-63163-579-3

Jolly Fish Press
North Star Editions, Inc.
2297 Waters Drive
Mendota Heights, MN 55120
www.jollyfishpress.com
Printed in Canada

For Cody, who would definitely choose camping over pencil sharpener sorting, and who would probably be right. And for Ellie, Abby, and David. Please always trust me with your lemon drops.

Chapter 1
AFTER

I keep telling myself it will all get easier next week.

Well . . . not *all*. The hardest part, I'm stuck with forever. But at least once school starts, I won't have to patrol this blazing playground every day like a sweaty prison guard, saving my siblings from death by monkey bars while Dad's at work.

Then again, who uses the word "easy" to describe junior high?

Manic giggling pulls my attention back to Janie and Budge—scrambling onto the zip line together like they *want* me to panic.

"One at a time, guys!"

"Pleeease, Morgan!" Janie leans dizzyingly far off the platform, her broomstraw hair sweeping the wood chips below. "We're practicing our trapeze act."

Familiar fear squirms in my gut. There's a good chance they're planning to construct an actual trapeze. Janie's seven-year-old brain is the source of all fun—for five-year-old Budge.

For their twelve-year-old sister?

"It's too dangerous."

Janie glares back at me.

I raise my eyebrows, channeling Mom. I can endure glaring to keep them in one piece.

But then she yells, "Mom would let us!"

I flinch. I don't know how many times this summer I've heard those words, and they never stop hurting.

Mom *would* let them.

Mom would do a million and one things better than I ever can.

"Fine."

It's not. But I can't bring myself to say what I'd have to say instead: Mom's gone. Mom won't ever be here again.

All you've got is me.

And Dad.

When he's home.

And when he can see us through The Fog.

The Fog rolled in after Mom died. It means a lot of the time Dad can't really see us, even when his eyes are pointed in our direction. It means when we talk, he asks us to repeat ourselves three times before he registers what we said. And when he tucks us in at night, there's no joking. No talking about our days. It's more like a robot replaced our real dad.

I should hate The Fog, but I'm scared that if it lifted, Dad would see how hard it is for me to hold everything together.

I wasn't supposed to be watching Budge and Janie all summer. At first it was just for one day until I found a way to convince Dad to make it just one week, then managed it again, over and over, because no matter how hard this is, it's better than the alternative.

I hold the zip line while they scramble up. It's only a few feet down if they fall, but I run alongside, gripping the back of Budge's faded red Mario shirt with claw-fingers.

"Let go," Janie begs. "Trapeze artists need to fly."

They do seem stable, but that's not the real reason I let them make the second run alone. I don't want to hear Janie say Mom would let them again.

I still watch, though—got to make sure they don't stand up, hang off, or basically attempt to die in any other way.

I wipe the sweat from my forehead with the back of my hand and shield my eyes as I tilt my face up to the washed-out sky. It's like all the blue has been erased by the burning afternoon sun, even though it's not directly overhead anymore.

"Hey, Morgan!" A voice calls from behind me. A voice I'd know anywhere.

Keilani.

A wave of regret washes over me, and I turn, even though I don't feel ready to see her.

She waves from the sidelines of the soccer field. She's wearing the US Women's World Cup Champion tee I gave her for her twelfth birthday. That should be comforting. If she's wearing my gift, maybe she hasn't totally given up on me as a friend.

Behind her, girls in cleats and shin guards warm up for soccer practice. My old team—Blue Thunder.

The new coach held tryouts at the end of May, back when all my family could do was cry.

I never even mentioned tryouts to Dad.

It's better this way. It's not like I have time for soccer anymore.

"Hey." We stare at each other across the green turf, like some magical force field keeps us from walking together and talking for real.

Keilani's been my best friend since we started pre-K soccer. Usually we spend all summer scrimmaging, playing cards, singing karaoke, or watching Star Wars with Hrishi—my next-door neighbor, and the third point in our best-friend triangle.

But nothing about this summer has been normal.

Mom had secret blood clots in her lungs that no one could see until she couldn't breathe anymore. She died in May, right before school got out.

Every day since, there's been a sad, stressed-out, parent-ish person where regular-old-kid Morgan used to be—After-Morgan. It's like I can't remember how to be anyone else.

Compared to losing Mom, none of the small stuff that's wrong in my life now should matter. I shouldn't still care what happened with Keilani that night in June when she and Mackelle brought brownies to my house.

Mackelle. Her name sounds like a fish. Like an exclamation of a fish.

Holy Mackelle! Why did I ever listen to you about anything?

Holy Mackelle! Why are you standing on my porch holding my mom's special brownies with *my* best friend?

I shift my feet, uncomfortable. The memory burns hotter than the August sun.

And Hrishi . . . I'm not even going to think about him. That can wait until he gets back from visiting his Nana and Nani in Mumbai. And talking about it can wait until approximately never. Ten fresh coats of industrial-grade paint wouldn't be enough to gloss over the awkwardness between us since Morgan's Stupidest Decision Ever.

To think I did it to *keep* my best friends together.

"How's it going?" Keilani tosses her thick, dark braid over her shoulder. She, of all people, should know how it's going. But I've only seen her a few times since Mom died.

"I'm fine!" I bellow the lie through the force field.

"Good to see you."

Good to see you? She sounds like somebody's grandma.

I should be glad she still wants to talk at all. I'll be extra glad next week when I'm wandering the halls of junior high, desperate for a friend to say, "How's it going?" and, "Good to see you." But with Keilani, small talk hurts worse than silence.

"Lani!" Mackelle waves Keilani over to partner up for a one-touch passing drill.

She shouldn't call her Lani. Keilani's proud of her name. Her dad says it means "royal one."

But "Lani" shrugs, teeth clenched in an apologetic smile, then runs off to join Mackelle.

Bam! Bam! Bam! The balls pound back and forth as the players kick them—precise and strong. Mackelle sends a bad pass, and the ball goes wide. That shouldn't make me smile. But I should be the one passing to Keilani. I wouldn't send it wide.

I rock forward on my toes, light and ready, like I could run for miles, dribbling the ball up and down the field.

I'm staring, wishing.

And suddenly, hoping.

I count the players at practice. Only twelve. They'll need eleven on the field at each game. Plus subs. Maybe they still need players. Maybe coach would understand if we told her why I wasn't at tryouts. Maybe—

A scream cuts through the air.

Budge!

I spin around.

The zip line swings empty, and Budge and Janie are nowhere. Not the swings, or the slide, or the tower where Janie always pretends to launch into space.

Then I hear Budge scream again, and my eyes find him.

He's hanging by one arm from the high monkey bars, looking way too small. I freeze for a moment before my legs remember how to run. Then I'm sprinting and panting and how did he get up that high in the first place and in a second he'll fall to the ground and break his legs or his head, and what if he's hurt so bad he'll never be okay again?

"Hold on, Budgie. I'll save you!" Janie shrieks, worming out over the monkey bars and reaching toward him.

But his fingers slip, and I can't reach him before he plunks to the ground like a stone.

Chapter 2

AFTER

I fall to my knees beside Budge, lying on his back in the wood chips.

"Are you hurt? Don't move." I slide my fingers through his blond curls, feeling his scalp for bumps or cuts.

He holds still for a second, like he's trying to figure out if he's wounded. Then his face crumples, and he starts to wail.

"Oh, no, Bud. Where does it hurt?" I reach for Mom's old phone that Dad makes me carry for emergencies. I still think of it as hers, not mine. At home it lives on the charging station—too much Mom to carry around in my pocket when I don't have to.

"I fell dowwwn." Big, drippy tears spill over his too-red cheeks.

"I know, Bud. I'm so sorry. I should have been watching you." I search with fumbling fingers for Dad's number, holding Budge in place with my other hand. He shouldn't move in case he hurt his head or neck.

"Morgan!" He sits up too fast for me to stop him, wood chips clinging to his tufty hair and shirt. "Do you want to play our game?" He scrubs his remaining tears away with one fist like he doesn't have time for them. "It's called tightrope, and you walk on the top of the monkey bars with your arms out so straight like this!" He demonstrates. "Like when Mario walks on those falling blocks in *Super Mario Galaxy*." Budge jumps to his feet, too excited to remember he just fell and could have broken his neck.

Which he didn't, apparently. My muscles go weak with relief, and I throw my arms around him.

Then his words sink in and I spin on Janie. "You guys walked on *top* of the monkey bars?"

She juts out her chin. "Every circus performer falls sometimes! He's just got to keep trying."

"Yeah. Watch me!" Budge starts toward the ladder.

"No!" I can't believe them. After what could have happened? "You can never, ever do that again. We're going home. Now!"

The anger in my voice is only partly at them. I was the one who looked away. Wishing for my old life distracted me, and it's my job to keep them safe.

The walk home is painful. Budge drags his feet until I'm practically carrying him. And Janie's posture speaks actual words.

Mean Morgan.

Bossy Morgan.

Enemy of Fun.

It's only after I promise she can make dinner that she'll speak to me.

"Really?" Her voice pierces the air like a ref's whistle.

I wince. "With help."

"Reallyreallyreallyreally?" She's probably still saying it, higher and higher, but now only dogs can hear her.

"And *after* we clean up. Dad could get home early."

She wrinkles her nose like she doesn't believe me.

Ha. I don't believe me either.

He always says he's planning to come home early. And I always tell him not to worry, that I've got this.

Either way, when Dad comes home to a mess, he feels guilty for leaving us home, and starts worrying about not doing enough for us, and after what he said to Grandma that one night . . . well, I'm not letting things get that out of control. It's not that hard to keep up with the house and dinners and babysitting so Dad won't do anything drastic to change our life even more.

Despite the upcoming forced tidying and unwelcome Morgan-help, Janie slips her hand into the one Budge isn't already holding. Mean Morgan forgotten.

It's a relief because my job is more than keeping them safe.

Mom used her last words to make sure I understood.

It was while she lay on the kitchen floor waiting for the ambulance, while Budge and Janie cried and begged her to get up, and dinner burned black on the stove. While I asked her over and over what she needed me to do.

Between gasps for air, she whispered, "Keep them safe, Morgan. Be brave for them. Help them be happy."

I promised.

And even if sometimes it seems impossible, at least I know she believed in me. And Dad and Budge and Janie depend on me to take care of all the things she used to handle so perfectly. I just have to try a little harder, and we'll all be okay.

I'm going to keep my promise to Mom.

Even if she didn't keep hers.

Chapter 3

BEFORE

In March, Hrishi helped my family cheer Blue Thunder to a 3-2 victory in our pre-season game with Rocky Mountain. When we returned home, Keilani was first out of our van and in through the garage door, singing "We Are the Champions" super loud.

Also super off-key.

Hrishi and I followed her into the kitchen, laughing.

"Keilani . . ." He ran his fingers through his pre-mussed dark hair. "You are a very nice and talented person. But if you want a musical career, you could consider an instrument. The clarinet, maybe. Or the tuba?"

She just sang louder in his face. Her tone deafness wasn't news to any of us. Hrishi's family owned an Indian restaurant with all-ages karaoke, and we'd been singing there together since Hrishi moved in next door when we were seven and demanded we change our best friend duo into a trio.

By the time Budge and Janie tromped inside, Keilani had already peeled a banana and was stuffing her face.

Mi casa was basically her *casa*. She'd already spent a lot of time at our house before her parents got divorced last summer, but since she'd chosen to stay with her dad when her big sister Tama moved out with their mom, Keilani had practically lived here.

"Me too." Budge pulled on her jersey until she peeled one for him and handed it over.

"Guys," she said around a mouthful of banana. "Did you *see* Morgan meg that girl in the second half? Sent the ball right through her giraffe legs." Keilani had some nerve, calling anybody out on their "giraffe legs." She was already like four inches taller than me.

"Like bulls-eying a womp rat in Beggar's Canyon." Hrishi nodded, solemnly.

"A womp rat?" I wrinkled up my nose at him. "What on earth, Hrishi?"

"It's a high compliment. Shooting womp rats?" He wrinkled his face at us. "Like Luke? On Tatooine? His training prep for hitting the two-meter target on the Death Star?"

"You're so weird," Keilani laughed.

She wasn't wrong. There were Star Wars fans, and then there were STAR WARS FANS. And then there was Hrishi—so steeped in galactic canon he made the rest look like indifferent ignoramuses.

"*I'm* weird. You're the ones acting like you've never seen *A New Hope*. Or you'd get that I'm agreeing you were awesome out there."

"Thanks." I covered my smile with my water bottle and let

the cool Gatorade slide down my throat. "Keilani set me up every time."

She was our best midfielder, always centering the ball perfectly for me to send it straight to net.

Now Hrishi pursed his lips, squinched up his face, his voice a growl-squeak. "With her today, the Force was."

"Thanks, Master Yoda." Keilani rolled her eyes. "But we couldn't have done it without Mackelle." She gave a low whistle. "Man, that girl can shoot!"

The smile slipped from my face. Mackelle played right forward, too, subbing in for me. She'd been training with our team since she moved here in February. Trying to hang out with me and Keilani too.

"She's okay." I shrugged. "But we don't even know if she'll make the team."

"I hope she does," Keilani said. "And we should be nice to her. Her family moves like every year or two, and it's hard making new friends everywhere she goes."

"I guess." I just wished Mackelle would stop explaining every tiny detail about junior high next year like she was some kind of coolness expert because where she lived in Washington, sixth grade was *middle school* and not babyish elementary. "I think she'd fit in better with Ellory and Diana than us."

"Who wants to hang out with Ellory and Diana?" Keilani wrinkled her nose like I said Mackelle should roll in a pile of garbage. "They're total divas."

I gave Keilani a look, waiting for her to catch up with me.

But she waved me away like an annoying fly. "Give her a chance," she said around a mouthful of banana. "We gave Hrishi a chance, and look how *that* turned out for us."

"Hey!" Hrishi punched her lightly in the arm. "Pretty sure *I* gave *you two* a chance."

We were laughing when Mom emerged from the garage, carrying her well-stocked game bag full of first aid supplies, extra water, and snacks.

"Thanks for the banana, Mama Bell." Keilani tossed her peel in the garbage. "Perfect recovery snack."

"Anytime. Just recover quickly so you girls can start on homework. Hrishi, you too. If you're sticking around, get to work." She grinned to soften it. But it wasn't like she was kidding.

I rolled my eyes at the two of them. There was a reason Hrishi and Keilani called her "Mama Bell." They were lucky Mom hadn't given them regular chores.

Janie took her backpack to the dining table without being asked. Mom's daily routines were . . . well . . . routine. But while Mom sat down at the kitchen desk to check off the day's events in ACTION, BACKUP, CLEANUP—the ABC planning calendar app she'd created for her life coaching business—Budge slunk out of the kitchen with two granola bars and without his backpack.

"Budge. After- school routine." Mom pointed without looking up at the color-coded poster where she'd broken all the chores and homework into manageable steps.

"Awww." Budge slumped. "I nevvver get to play *Mario* anymore now that I'm in preschool."

"Your time, your choice." Mom's tone was neutral. "Plan wisely, and you'll have free time."

"But—"

"Benjamin Michael." She raised an eyebrow to punctuate her use of Budge's "real" name. Unless he was in trouble, he'd been "Budge" ever since he was born, when two-year-old Janie's best attempt at his name was "Budge-Man."

Mom waited for a squirming Budge-Man to meet her eyes before she went on. "Plan A is to cooperate the first time you're asked. Then you'll be free to decide what you do next. Should we move to Plan B?"

She didn't even mention Plan C—CLEANUP—which would probably involve a tantrum and some cool-off time.

In our house, we almost never hit Plan C, since Mom said the goal was to live life in those first two columns. Plan C was the place where you cleaned up the mess life became if you didn't make Plans A and B work.

Budge shook his head, but before heading to tidy his room, he paused to write on his fridge-magnet whiteboard in wobbly caps.

I HAT CHORz

I laughed out loud. I felt his pain.

Mom gave me a look. "I'm serious, Morgan. Get on your afternoon routine. I need you to supervise Budge and Janie while I teleconference with a client in half an hour, and then I've got to prep for a video I'm recording for the ABC Channel."

"Dang, Morgan." Keilani laughed. "Mama Bell's a machine. She can solve all the world's problems in like fifteen minutes."

True. But it wasn't always easy being the child of the ABC planning guru. Her devoted in-person clients and hundred thousand online followers looked to her—some even paid her—to manage their lives. We got it all for free whether we liked it or not.

But that reminded me. Today, Keilani herself needed some of that Mama Bell magic. Hopefully before Mom's client session. This was a perfect segue.

"She *can* solve those problems," I said. "Speaking of, didn't you say you needed a *lemon drop*?" I grabbed the blue willow crock of lemon drops from its place on the counter next to the sugar and flour and other staple ingredients of our everyday life and slid it to her across the island.

In our house when someone said *"lemon drop"* all heavy like that, they meant more than just candy. Mom always said difficult conversations were like lemon drops—sour at first, but soon becoming sweet, easier to handle.

"Ooh, a *lemon drop*? I'm in!" Hrishi snatched a powdery candy from the jar and popped it in his mouth. Then he leaned both elbows on the island, dramatically rubbing his hands together. "What are we talking about?"

"Keilani needs—"

But what Keilani needed at the moment was apparently to elbow me in the stomach, yank furiously on her left braid, and stare at her feet, while blotches of red climbed her neck.

What . . . Oh!

She didn't want to talk in front of Hrishi.

Like he was a *boy*, instead of plain old Hrishi.

Just a couple of years ago we all used to change out of our swim clothes in the backyard without thinking about it, and last year after Human Growth and Development Day, when Hrishi demanded details from the girl class, Keilani was the first to spill. Hrishi's mind was blown when he found out girls also grow armpit hair.

But Keilani was still studying her shoes like they were the reason her face was on fire.

"Uh, Hrishi . . . don't you need to get home for . . . dinner?" I stammered.

"Naw, I'm good." He grabbed another lemon drop, oblivious.

Mom stood up from her desk, joining us at the island. She always made time for a lemon drop.

"Keilani?" Mom raised one super-expressive eyebrow.

"Um . . ."

We all waited. Mom with her eyebrow, Keilani tugging on her long, black braids, and me, boring a hole in Hrishi with my eyeballs.

Hrishi darted his gaze between the three of us. "Why do I get the feeling y'all are trying to get rid of me?"

I shrugged, smiling apologetically.

"Okay. Cool, cool." He slow-nodded. "Girl time it is. Hrishi out." He fist-bumped all three of us.

"Yup. Scram." Keilani acting like herself again was a relief. We all laughed as Hrishi slunk out through the back screen door like a ninja.

"So?" Mom said.

Keilani still had a hint of pink tinging her cheeks as she took three lemon drops from the crock, putting them in her mouth in exaggerated slow motion. She puckered up, tasting three times the sour all at once.

We waited in silence until the hum of the fridge grew deafening, while Keilani eyed the back door like she half expected Hrishi to still be lurking behind it.

"Okay." She cleared her throat. "The thing is, Mama Bell . . . and I hope you can handle it. We're going to be talking about boobs today."

She looked Mom in the eyes then, as if daring her to react.

Mom blinked, hesitated only a second, then said, "I can't believe you! Are you saying I can't handle it because I have no boobs of my own?"

There was a stunned silence, while all three of us looked awkwardly at Mom's flattish chest.

Then Keilani started laughing right from her belly, self-consciousness gone that fast. Mom and I joined her, and pretty soon, Mom was wiping away tears.

When Keilani could breathe again, she said, "Yeah, we need to talk about *my* boobs. Because *I* actually have some. And they're in trouble. Like, seriously. It's Bra-pocalypse."

Which just started us off again.

I shook my head. Mom might be embarrassing. But she also knew what people needed. When to tease Keilani. When to hold my hand and help me breathe through anxiety. When to let Budge deal with the consequences of his own lack of time management.

"Well played." Mom laughed. "But seriously, now. What's up with your boobs?"

Just like that, Keilani was talking about developing faster than anyone on our team, and how *seriously* uncomfortable it was bouncing all over the soccer field—even though Keilani was sure Mom would have no idea—and how with her mom and Tama living an hour away she was stuck with her dad, who went to the store and told the sales girl, who was apparently a D cup, that his daughter was "about her size."

"When I asked him to take me back for one that fits, he said . . ." Keilani pulled her chin into her neck like a turtle, her voice going deep, "'Can't you stuff socks in the one I already bought you and give God some time?'"

By this point we were dying. Dy. Ing.

"Sure, laugh," Keilani moaned. "Enjoy my pain."

"Oh, Keilani." Mom wiped tears from her eyes. "Your poor dad. Men were never meant to do this on their own, bless their hearts. You sure you can't ask your mom?"

Keilani shook her head a little too fast.

"Got it." Mom had on her business face as she grabbed her phone and fired up her app. "What you need is an excellent ABC plan."

I rolled my eyes. "I think Plan A will get the job done."

This time Mom turned her eyebrows on me. "*Plan A* was socks in the bra. We've got to fix . . . *Bra-pocalypse*. We can't have Keilani jiggling down the soccer pitch, and besides, you girls start junior high in the fall. A girl can't go to junior high without a real, properly fitting bra, no matter how many socks she uses." She poised her pointer finger above the B column in the planning app. "Any ideas for Plan B? You always need a good Plan B."

I almost rolled my eyes again, but then I saw the grin on Keilani's face, and remembered why we talked to Mom about this in the first place. Why we always did.

Her ABC plans might be annoying, but Mom could turn an Anything-pocalypse into a little less of a disaster.

Chapter 4

AFTER

It's been six months since Plan B for Bra-pocalypse, and at least three months since Keilani's been inside our house at all. She'd die if she could see our kitchen in its current post–Mama Bell state. She'd call it "Food-pocalypse" for sure. I'm still scrubbing today's crusty peanut butter and jelly glue off the counter when Janie bursts into the kitchen.

"Finished tidying! I'm going online for a new recipe."

No way I'm letting her fill this nearly clean island with pots, crumbs, and slime.

"Make something quick and simple."

She wrinkles her nose like I suggested liver and steamed spinach.

"Soup," I suggest. "Or tuna sandwiches, or—"

"Spaghetti!" She claps. "And the garlic toast flowers in muffin cups."

I stop wiping and squeeze the rag so hard it drips onto the counter. "We're out of spaghetti."

"Why are we aaalllways out of spaghetti?" she moans.

We were supposed to have spaghetti May third, the day Mom died.

By the time I got back inside from seeing Mom off with the ambulance, the noodles were ash, glued to the bottom of the pot. We threw out the pot, and the next week I threw out all the spaghetti.

It's Janie's favorite, but I'm not cooking it. Not now. Not ever.

I suck in a deep breath like my therapist Alejandro showed me. He says it sends calming dopamine right to my brain.

Before Mom died, I'd seen him a few times for what he called "generalized anxiety." Like when I had trouble sleeping in fifth grade, or when I stressed out before a big soccer tournament. But Dad made me go back when I had my first panic attack after Mom died. For a few sessions at least. Until I got things back together.

It's not that I don't like Alejandro. I do. He's way big on taking control of our own brain chemistry. I'm way big on not having meltdowns where anyone can see. We make a pretty good team.

It's just . . . needing to show your dad you're okay and weekly therapy visits *don't* make that great of a team.

I scan the fridge for dinner options. Yogurt, butter, milk, and a few wrinkled apples.

I sigh, closing the fridge. Mom used to clean it off weekly, but no one has bothered in months. Tucked into the chaos of magnets and pizza coupons, Dad's note stares at me, written on a blue-lined sticky note from Mom's command center.

It's a couple of months old, edges curling up, and splattered with dried blue droplets—probably from when Budge dropped his carefully melted freeze-pop soup a few weeks ago.

Dad wrote it the first day he left us home alone. The day after my first panic attack.

MORGAN,

YOU'RE A TROOPER FOR TAKING CARE OF THINGS TODAY. I PROMISE YOU WON'T NEED TO BABYSIT FOR LONG. I'VE GOT A COUPLE MORE CALLS TO MAKE TO FIND SOMEONE TO HELP OUT, AND I'M SORRY TO LEAVE YOU LIKE THIS. I'LL BE HOME EARLY FROM WORK TO MAKE DINNER. CALL IF YOU NEED ANYTHING.

—DAD

Even though the words don't say how worried he was because of what had happened the night before, it's clear in each careful block letter.

And the message is still true. If I can't ease that worry, he'll try to make life better for us, making things so much worse.

I crumple the note into the trash, and search the cupboards.

"Chili?" I hold out two cans with a hopeful smile.

"But—"

"With baked potatoes?"

"But that's so boooring."

"Not if you make something out of the potatoes. Stack them up like . . . a mountain?" A burst of inspiration hits me. "Like a volcano with chili for the lava!"

It's the chili lava that wins her over. She bounces over to the can opener.

I sigh in relief.

Short-lived relief.

Budge picks that moment to race into the kitchen and yank my arm half out of its socket.

"Stop!" I pry him off. "Is your room tidy?"

He shakes his head solemnly. "First I need a lemon drop."

"They're all gone," I say.

It's a lie.

I hid them. Behind the camping dishes. And I need them to stay there—buried in the cabinet where they can't hurt me.

Chapter 5

AFTER

(But only by a few weeks)

After Mom died, lemon drops went straight from everyday comfort to a thing of the past.

For the first three weeks, Dad mostly just stared into the distance with red-rimmed eyes, but at least the warm space under his arm was always available for someone who needed to nudge their way in and stay there, silently borrowing his strength.

Tomorrow, though, Dad was going back to work.

Of course he was. He couldn't stay home with us forever.

Because bills, and groceries, and house payments.

Because life.

That was the worst part.

We were supposed to just do life again, like nothing had changed?

At first it was just a little tug in my stomach, like the beginning of the flu or the end of too much junk food.

But then I yelled at Budge for singing the Mario theme song. And I couldn't swallow more than three bites of dinner. I stopped talking because I felt hot and cold and shaky, like maybe my churning stomach was the beginning of some terrible disease that would mean Dad couldn't go back tomorrow, and I could just lie on the couch and watch cartoons while he brought me sports drinks and checked my temperature.

Except I didn't need electrolytes and thermometers.

What I needed was a lemon drop.

I needed it like I needed food I couldn't eat, water I couldn't drink.

Air I couldn't breathe.

When Dad found me after dinner, I was huddled in a ball on my bed, shaking and holding my knees so tight, while I struggled to get oxygen into my lungs. Which didn't make any sense because that probably squeezed my lungs and made it harder to breathe.

But nothing made any sense that night.

Dad was going back to work.

We were all going back to life.

And there were no lemon drops because there was no Mom, which meant what could life even be?

It took him a while to get me untangled, whispering soft, soothing, meaningless words while he maneuvered me into his arms like a baby so he could smooth my sweat-drenched hair, stroke my tear-stained face, and rock me back and forth. He even sang "Edelweiss," Mom's special song for me.

"What can I do?" he asked when I finally remembered how to pull air in and out of my lungs. "What do you need?"

It was a long time before I could whisper back, "A lemon drop."

He listened to everything, just like Mom used to. He patted my back and my hair. He promised to be home tomorrow as early as he could possibly get away, and that he'd work out something better as soon as he could.

He wrapped me up in as much safety and peace as I could feel, three weeks after losing Mom. I even thought for a few drowsy minutes that I had done the right thing telling him everything.

But later that night, I woke to the sound of him crying. Real crying.

When I tiptoed down the hall to his bedroom to find out what was wrong, he was on the phone, talking between sobs with his head in his hands. I'd never seen a grown-up cry like that.

I knew I shouldn't eavesdrop, but all the safety and peace from our lemon drop drained away, gluing my feet in place.

"I can't—" His voice broke. "I don't even know how to start doing this without her. I don't think I can." He stopped talking as his shoulders shook.

Eventually he sniffed, ran a hand over his eyes. "I don't know," he said. "I thought they were doing . . . I don't know . . . fine, I guess. Not good, of course, because—" A sob tore out of him. "You should have heard her, Mom."

Mom.

Grandma Bell on the phone from Michigan. She'd gone home the day after the funeral because Grandpa's Parkinson's made leaving him difficult. It was okay. They lived so far away that we'd never gotten to spend much time with them.

But she was Dad's Mom. *His* Mom was still alive. And right now he was having his own lemon drop.

"She was curled up in her bed shaking. Totally . . . collapsing."

One word flew toward me. Hit me square in the chest—*she*. Dad was talking about me.

"I know." He sniffed loudly. "But with Dad's health, you guys moving out here? It's not even an option." Another sob rolled out of him, low and desperate. I wanted to run to him, put my arms around him, and make everything all better.

I wanted to undo the lemon drop and make him un-know all those feelings that had poured out of me all over him.

"I'm barely holding my head above water." His voice was almost a whisper, and I had to strain to hear his next words. "Things are heating up at work again, especially with me gone these three weeks. We need a babysitter. But child care is expensive, and after funeral expenses, and with the loss of Eve's income . . ."

The loss of Eve's income. I held my breath for a second. I'd never even thought about the money Mom's clients used to pay her to help them fix their lives.

And a babysitter? Some stranger in our house, doing things Mom used to do. Things I could do better myself? I'd been watching Budge and Janie by myself for a year, now, for errands or date nights.

Dad turned his head, and I shrank back from the door. I didn't want him to see me, seeing him with the weight of the whole world pressing down on him.

"Believe me. I've thought about it," he said. "Living this far from family has made things . . . yeah . . . It's just I worry about what a move would do to them, Mom."

A move?

"It's got to be a last resort. If they lose their home and their friends at this point . . ."

A shiver started at my head, washing goose bumps down my shoulders and arms.

Lose their home? Their friends?

Was Dad really considering moving us away?

I started to shake as my stomach turned to ice.

We couldn't move away from our home. From the place that held every memory of Mom. From a chance to fix things with Keilani and Hrishi.

Everything, *everything* could change for the worse. For all of us. And it would be my fault. I promised Mom I'd be brave for them, help them be happy. Told her I'd be the solution, not the problem.

My teeth started to chatter, and I felt my arms and legs straining to curl me up in a ball right here on the floor. Where Dad could find me.

No.

I clamped my teeth together. I had to be stronger than that.

Keep them safe, Morgan. Be brave for them. Help them be happy. That's what Mom said.

That's what I promised.

And that's what I was going to do.

When I saw Dad's sticky note message waiting on the fridge the next day, I made sure that no matter how early he got home from work, he'd see dinner made, the house clean.

That day, and every day after, I showed him we were fine without the sitter we couldn't afford. Promised I'd call if we had a problem.

But I made sure we never had any. I showed everyone smiling, happy Morgan, and kids who had everything they needed.

I stood tippy-toed on a stool to hide those lemon drops away in the cupboard behind the camping dishes that we wouldn't be using anytime soon. Told myself I didn't need them anymore.

Couldn't need them was probably closer to the truth, but it didn't make much difference.

Chapter 6

AFTER

"No. I need a *lemon drop*." Budge's eyes bug out of his head, he's so serious.

I take a deep breath.

For a while after that night with Dad I still tried to have lemon drops with Mom in my mind.

Everyone needs a lemon drop every now and then. It's what she always said.

I'd suck on a lemon drop and take both sides of the conversation—me talking, with the hint of what she would have said echoing in my mind.

The candy would turn sweet, but talking to Almost-Mom never did. Even now, the thought fills my mouth with saliva, puckering my lips like I'm tasting the sour.

I sigh. "Okay. But for real, the candy is gone," I lie again. "And sit at the island, so I can finish dinner." I dump the potatoes into the sink, each one thudding right onto my nerves.

"So *we* can finish dinner." Janie struggles to clamp the can opener onto the chili.

"Fiiine." Budge squirms up onto the stool. I'm not sure whether he's madder about the missing candy or the public lemon drop. "Okaaay. Here's my lemon drop." He cranes his neck toward me so I won't miss his theatrically serious expression. "I'm super-*duper* scared to start school."

You and me both.

I look out the kitchen window at Hrishi's dark blinds, pulled closed all summer while he's away. I'm not sure whether to be glad or terrified that he's coming back next week. And then there's Keilani, split from me by that force field . . . permanently?

Mackelle said everything would change. I hated her for it—still do. But it looks like she was right. And starting school without my perfectly balanced Keilani-Hrishi-Morgan triangle?

"What if I don't like it? What if they never let me play *Mario* and go to the park? What if math is too hard because I only know plusses and some minuses and not any of the timeses, except five times five equals twenty-five?"

I scrub fiercely at the potatoes.

What if my best friends aren't talking to me?

What if I can't make new friends because instead of playing soccer and hanging out after school I'm making dinner and babysitting and deep breathing to avoid a panic attack?

What if I need a lemon drop every night of junior high, and for me, there won't ever be lemon drops again?

"Morgan!" Budge slaps his hand on the counter, snapping me out of my daze.

The potato I'm holding looks flaky and weird. I've scrubbed off most of the peel.

"Are you even listening to my lemon drop?" His voice is indignant.

"School will be fun," I say brightly. "You can already read and write, so you're basically ready to teach kindergarten."

"Teach kindergarten," Budge cracks up.

"You'll love school!" Janie glops the chili into the sauce-pan. "There's gym, and recess, and after-school activities, like my dance classes. What sport will you pick, Budgie? Also, you get new clothes, and backpacks, and Mom writes notes on our napkins in our . . ." Her eyes widen as she realizes this year her lunch box will have no napkin notes.

Not unless I find a way to fit that in too.

I start stabbing damp potatoes with a steak knife so they won't explode in the microwave.

Who is going to tell them this is so much bigger than lunch box notes?

Stab.

Who will tell Janie that no parent available to drive me to soccer means no one to take her to dance lessons either?

Stab.

Who will tell them to stop needing things or Dad might have to move us across the country, where we'll never see our friends or our house or anything familiar again?

Stab.

Who will tell them life is one hundred percent different now? Forever.

Stab. Stab. Stab.

Wouldn't want the pressure to build up inside these potatoes, and then . . . boom.

Janie is suddenly standing at my elbow, nudging me like a cat in need of affection. I put down the knife and slip an arm around her without looking down at her face.

Maybe no one needs to tell them after all.

"Everything will be great," I say in a cartoon princess voice as I pull away from Janie to finish the potatoes. "Don't worry."

"But school starts in a week," Janie says in a small voice. "And we're not ready."

She's right. Dad hasn't said a word about back-to-school prep.

I slide a finger around the too-tight waistband of my denim shorts. Over the summer I've gotten curvier everywhere, and none of my clothes fit right anymore. Not to mention I'm still wearing the training bras Mom bought last fall.

A girl can't go to junior high without a real, properly fitting bra, no matter how many socks she uses.

The wild laugh that bubbles up at the memory of Keilani's dad and the bra socks dies in my throat. I'd already have that bra if I hadn't been so stupid.

"I'm sure Dad will take us this week." My hands shake as I put the murder victim potatoes into the microwave.

But I'm *not* sure.

I've spent the last two months showing Dad how hundred percent certainly I've got this, and he's pretty much gone back to business as usual. Like Mom is still here, invisibly doing everything she used to do. Which I guess means I've been doing a good job so far, but makes me doubt he's thought of back-to-school.

My voice is shaky when I say, "Why don't you guys jump on the trampoline until dinner's ready?"

Budge runs for the back door, lemon drop forgotten that quickly.

Janie hesitates. "What about the volcanoes?"

"I'll call you as soon as the potatoes are done." *Please. Just go.*

"Promise?"

"Promise."

I hate that word. But it gets her out the door.

The ground spins under me, as I watch the hissing potatoes turn in circles, releasing their own pressure.

For the first time in my life, I'm jealous of food.

Chapter 7
BEFORE

I was at the dining table doing homework when Mom burst in, arms full of bulky canvas prints.

I dropped my pen and hurried to help her stabilize the teetering stack. "What's all this?"

"Thanks, Morgan Beth." Her smile lit her whole face. "It's a surprise for Dad. I printed the best pictures he took on our Capitol Reef trip last summer. Help me hang them before he gets home for dinner?"

When Mom had a project, she didn't wait. Not unless The Plan said otherwise.

We worked together with the level and the tape measure, fulfilling the vision Mom had in her head. Before long the prints formed a rough circle on the wall.

Cohab Canyon, Castle Rock, Fruita Campground, Cassidy Arch. A colorful mosaic of red rocks and blue skies and summer-green cottonwoods.

A flood of memory washed over me—our family, together in our favorite place on earth. Setting up our campsite, working our way carefully over a waterfall, shielding our eyes from the sunlight reflecting off Sulphur Creek. Picking peaches and apples in the orchards. Reading in hammocks that swayed in the breeze.

"Dad will love it." I picked up my pencil to complete my fractions assignment.

"He *does* love it." Dad's laughing voice surprised us both, and we turned.

"Dad!" I threw my arms around him for a hug, and he picked me up and spun me around.

"Oof," he groaned. "You're getting too old for this."

"Never." I laughed. "Just be glad I don't walk up your stomach so I can flip anymore."

He shook out his arms like I'd completely exhausted his strength, then pulled Mom in for a kiss.

"Not like I'm going to complain about you getting home early," Mom said when they finished totally grossing me out, "but this was a surprise, and you caught me before I could add the finishing touch." She tried to cover his eyes with her hand, but he dodged around her and kissed her again.

Okay, so not *totally* finished grossing me out. But knowing my parents, the grossing out would last approximately forever.

She wiggled out of Dad's embrace and pulled the final canvas from a bright orange Crafter's Corner bag.

The sign had some cutesy font with the words, "If you fail to plan, you are planning to fail."

She held the "finishing touch" in place. "Here, or a little lower?"

"That's perfect," Dad said.

"Isn't it?" Mom took a step away, sighing with satisfaction. "What do you think, Morgan?" She bumped me with her arm.

"It's . . . nice?"

Mom laughed. "Tell me how you really feel."

"How *I* really feel is that this is the best photo display you've put together yet." Dad planted a kiss on the top of her head. "Just the sight of it makes me want to pack us up and drive straight to Capitol Reef. What do you say, Eve? This weekend?"

"Wait, what? Are you serious?" I did an excited little jump before I could stop myself.

"The kids have school, and it's a long drive. Plus we already have our trip scheduled in June like always," Mom said in her reasonable tone.

"Please, Mom? Pleasepleasepleaseplease?" My voice rose like when Hrishi and Keilani and I sucked all that helium out of his birthday balloons last month. And staring at the colorful pictures on the wall, my head started floating like the balloons, pre-helium-suckage.

"Yeah, Mom. Pleasepleasepleaseplease." Dad gave her puppy eyes.

Mom shook her head. "We've got soccer games. Morgan and Keilani have a late-night planned. If we want to move our trip up closer, go check the calendar and see if you can find a time when it would work. For everyone."

All the spontaneous campout helium splurted out of me, and I sagged right back to earth. She was too good at making the calendar the bad guy. It was always "The Plan" saying no. Never Mom.

"The sign doesn't really fit there," I said.

Mom turned her eyes on me, mouth turning down. "We needed something in the middle," she said. "There was a hole."

"Yeah, but it should be another picture." I folded my arms, channeling my frustration at Mom's wall display. "Like your rainbow hammock or Gifford Farmhouse or something."

Dad slipped in between us, draping an arm around her shoulder, and squeezing my arm with his other hand. "The wall is like your mom and me—a perfect balance."

Mom glanced over at me and I made a half-hearted attempt at a smile.

"We'll go in June." Dad gave my arm another double-squeeze. "We'll have a great time, *and* follow The Plan. In the meantime, I'll check the calendar to see about scheduling us a day hike, since we are obviously in need of an adventure."

Mom leaned gratefully into Dad, and I gathered up my homework, leaving them to their *perfect balance*, still quietly mourning the loss of a spontaneous camping trip, and resenting the bossy sign in the center of our wall.

ABC Planning. Blah.

I mean, it wasn't *all* bad. I was cool with Plan A. Plan A meant knowing what you wanted, and going to get it.

It was Plan B I had a problem with.

Plan B was what was left over when everything you wanted was gone.

And Plan C? Not even an option.

Chapter 8

AFTER

I stare at Mom's Capitol Reef display—the pictures seeming to fade until the black-and-white words in the middle are all I can see.

Did she hang this then because she somehow knew I'd need a nudge right now?

I may hate ABC planning, but I don't hate how it made our lives work. Someone needs to weave our loose threads together before we unravel completely.

My eyes burn, and I blink quickly. I will not cry. Red, puffy eyes will only make Dad worry.

Mom's phone sits quietly at the charging station, waiting for me.

I was always her secretary while she drove, responding to texts, narrating the daily plan, changing events in the ABC columns of her app's tidy calendar.

For the first time since Mom died, I fire up ACTION, BACKUP, CLEANUP, and stare down at the last plan she ever made.

MAY 3RD

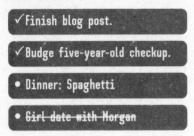

✓ Finish blog post.

✓ Budge five-year-old checkup.

● Dinner: Spaghetti

● ~~Girl date with Morgan~~

A searing pain grips my chest, and I almost put the phone down.

No.

I can do this.

I can plan the best possible life for us, like Mom would if she were here. But first, I've got to erase her old plan. I can't scroll forward, find out what she had planned for May fourth, fifth, and forever that never happened.

> **Reset**
>
> Do you want to erase your plan? This cannot be undone.

My finger hesitates.

"Want" is the absolutely wrong word, but there's not an option for when you *have to* erase your plan.

I press my finger firmly down on the bright green YES, and today's date pops up, starting with this very hour, divided into three columns—ACTION, BACKUP, CLEANUP.

I'm about to fill in the Plan A space with what I'm doing right now: make plan.

But it feels wrong. Plan A was that Mom would be with us.

No matter how hard we try, we won't ever be in Plan A again.

I laugh, a short, bitter burst. I always hated BACKUP plans anyway. Two columns are more than enough, because I'm going to make sure my first plan works.

I enter "make plan" in the BACKUP column, and an odd feeling of relief washes over me. Even with the looming threat of Plan B being only one step away from Plan C, at least we're moving in the right direction.

I might actually succeed, if I don't try to turn this plan into something it can never be.

Chapter 9

AFTER

Dad gets home at six—early for him these days. His face looks weird, and I stare at him a second.

He's smiling. Like, real smiling. The kind that starts in the eyes, instead of the mouth—like The Fog has lifted. I can't remember the last time he looked like that. Can he already sense how my plan will make things better?

"Daddy, Daddy!" Budge leaps up for a hug.

"Budge-Man!" Dad spins him around. Janie demands a turn too.

When I don't demand a spin of my own, Dad pats me awkwardly on the shoulder.

"Thanks for making dinner again."

"*I* made dinner," Janie corrects him. "*Almost* all by myself. Come eat!"

Dad's smile falters when he looks down at his plate.

"Chili volcanoes," I prompt him. He'd never have guessed on his own.

I was so absorbed planning the coming week down to the last shopping trip, back-to-school night, and Locker-Textbook-Palooza that I didn't hear the microwave timer. Apparently sitting extra-long in a hot, moist microwave turns overstabbed potatoes to mush, and Janie had to stabilize her food sculptures with many toothpicks. The result is a cross between slaughtered porcupine and spiny vomit.

"Erupting beautifully." Dad winks at me. "Thanks, Janie."

She beams as he takes a careful, spine-avoidant bite.

"Is *not* beautiful," Budge mutters, holding up his special notebook so we can all read his verdict, captured in wonky block letters: **THS CHILY IS DEE SGUS DING.**

Ha. He's worried about kindergarten academics? Even in kid spelling, Budge can certainly get his point across.

"Budge!" Janie glares at Dad, waiting for him to tell Budge off.

"Say sorry, Bud." Dad chokes back a laugh.

"Sorry, Bud." Budge grins, making Janie shriek with rage.

"This is delicious," I say quickly, desperate to placate Janie. Dad's great mood won't last long if he's refereeing an all-out Budge-and-Janie brawl. The Fog could roll right back in, and I'll never be able to bring up my plan. "Dad—"

"I need to talk to you all about something," he says.

"Something fun?" Janie's body vibrates like she's conducting an electric current, and I lean away, like her touch will zap me.

"Very fun. But it's coming up soon, and it'll take lots of prep. I'll need to go shopping, and Morgan can help get your clothes ready. We'll all have to pitch in."

Shopping? Get our clothes ready?

Dad remembered back-to-school?

Relief drops my shoulders about three inches. I don't have

to do this all on my own. And he'll love my plan. It'll only make things easier.

"Exactly," I say. "I've been planning—"

"We're going to spend next week camping in Capitol Reef. We'll leave Saturday," Dad announces.

His words freeze me in place.

Saturday? That's . . . the day after tomorrow.

Janie jumps up and down. "Camping? In Capitol Reef? Really?"

Budge stands on his chair, leaning so far across the table, he's about to fall into Dad's chili volcano. "Wait! Is that the one where we eat ice cream at the farm?"

My head spins, dizzy.

"Yes!" Janie exults. "Gifford Farmhouse Ice Cream! Can we do all our favorite hikes, and roast marshmallows, and watch stars at night?"

"Sure!" Dad grins.

Budge leaps from his chair, racing around the table like that kid in *The Incredibles*.

I look across the room at the photos of Capitol Reef, where Mom's sign is practically yelling at me.

If you fail to plan, you are planning to fail.

"Morgan," Dad says. "You okay? It's just our regular Capitol Reef trip like every summer."

But that's just it.

This is not every summer.

It's *this* one—irreparably different than any summer before.

I guess I didn't expect our family to do things like camping anymore. Like without Mom, all special occasions would be canceled forever.

And my plan . . .

Mom would have squashed this, directed his attention to The Plan—the polar opposite of his spontaneous chaos.

I'd have been jumping up and down and rooting for Dad.

But Mom's not here. So instead, Budge and Janie do the jumping-up-and-downing, while I sit like a statue, my careful lists scrolling through my mind, a bold line striking each item through.

~~Real bras~~

~~School supplies~~

~~Locker-Textbook-Palooza~~

If Dad thinks we can pull this trip off in two days, he has no clue how much organizing, cooking, and packing Mom did behind the scenes. Once we get there, who will rein in his hiking before we collapse from dehydration or fall off a cliff? And when the trip falls apart without Mom, how will I hide my anxiety with Dad watching me every minute of the day?

My hands shake, and I squeeze them together in my lap.

"We can't go this week." My voice is a whisper, so I clear my throat. Try again, louder. "There's too much to do. We have to—"

"Capitol Reef! Capitol Reef!" Budge and Janie's chanting drowns out my words, drumming on my nerve endings that seem to stick out three inches above my skin. Budge leans so close drops of spit from the "f" in "Reef" hit my face.

"No!" I shout. "We can't go camping! Not next week."

Silence follows my outburst, except for my pulse, rushing in my ears.

"Daaad," Janie wails. "Is she right?"

"No." His tone is firmer than it's been since before Mom died, but then he says, more softly, "You okay, Morgan?"

"Yeah. Sorry." A sharp pain throbs behind my eyes. "But we really can't go right now. School starts in a week, and we need to buy clothes and supplies, find out our new schedules, meet the teachers. I've made a whole plan, right here." I hold up Mom's phone.

"That's great," Dad says cheerfully. "But we can do both—have a relaxing camping trip, and then follow your plan—it's the perfect balance." He moves his open palms up and down like scales. "We'll be back two days before school starts," he says in a slow, reasonable voice. "In plenty of time to buy binders and . . . eraser sharpeners and whatnot."

Eraser sharpeners? He really can't be in charge of the plan.

"Hooray!" Janie hug-strangles him, possibly shattering his eardrum as well. "This is the best day of my liiife so far! Come on, Budge! Let's pack!"

They run off, and Dad shakes his head, laughing.

I can't join him. A giant hand is squeezing my chest.

I wish I could be like Janie—certain that even on the best day of her life, better days are coming.

"You need a break." Dad's eyes focus in like brain-deciphering

X-rays. "You've been working way harder than anyone your age should. Acting like a mini adult. And I should have—"

"No, Dad—" I break off, unsure how to finish that sentence. Not like I can tell him the reason I'm a mini adult is so he won't notice anything's wrong and make things even worse than they are by trying to fix them.

"Morgan, I think you need this—"

"But—"

"*We* need this." His voice is hoarse with emotion.

I look up at Mom's colorful wall display, so perfectly capturing Dad's favorite place.

He needs this.

"It's been a . . ." He pauses to clear his throat. "A really hard summer for everyone, and we need to reset before we start a difficult fall. We can't stop living because—" He breaks off, but the sentence finishes itself in my mind like Budge himself spelled it out in his notebook.

We can't stop living because Mom did.

My silence makes the line between his eyebrows deepen, but I don't trust my voice to answer.

"It's just camping," he says. "We've done it a million times. If we work together, we've got this. And we'll do all the important parts of your plan when we get back, okay? Anyway, the point of plans is flexibility. What do they say? Life is what happens when you're busy making other plans?" He smiles hopefully.

I want to ask him what that even means. I hate sentences

that sound like they should be framed in the middle of a display of camping photos. But I don't ask. I already know.

It means we're going camping.

Chapter 10

BEFORE

Last summer as we rolled into Torrey—the barely there tourist town outside Capitol Reef—six-year-old Janie gasped herself awake.

"Red! I see red!" She strained against her seat belt between me and Keilani, squeezing our arms with vise-grip hands. Her hair was a bird's nest from using us as pillows the whole drive. "Red rocks mean we're almost there."

"That's right." Mom turned around. "Keilani, I'm so glad you came this year."

"Me too." Keilani's voice was subdued. "My mom says thanks for having me. It made things lots easier for her and Dad."

I looked over, checking if she was okay, but she kept her eyes on the rock shops and restaurants and motels passing by her window.

"I can't believe this is your first time camping," I said.

"Yeah. What will we be doing, exactly?"

"Hiking every minute we're awake," Dad said brightly.

Keilani's eyes widened.

Mom laughed. "The first time I hiked with Josh, none of my muscles worked the next day. When my roommate asked how I'd enjoyed the trip, I told her, 'I pity the fool who winds up with that man.'"

"Ha. Ha." Dad said the words instead of laughing them.

"Obviously you got over it." Keilani sounded more like herself.

"I'd say so." Mom grinned. "But don't worry. I won't let him force march you all week. We'll also be lying in hammocks, playing in the river, and reading amazing books."

"You're going to love it," I whispered.

Keilani smiled back at me, and I really hoped I wasn't lying. Really hoped she could love anything right then.

At that very moment, her mom was home with Tama, putting their things into boxes. Moving out of the house where Keilani was going to stay with her dad. Moving too far for Keilani to jump back and forth a week at a time.

Keilani said she couldn't leave her dad. Said otherwise who would make sure he didn't eat boiled potatoes for every meal?

But it was more than that.

Her dad was actually around. Her mom hadn't been for a long time.

"Wake up, Budgie," Janie squealed. "We're here!"

As we turned out of Torrey, Capitol Reef spread in front of us like a red, blue, and green watercolor in the morning sun.

"Wow," Keilani breathed.

I grinned at her. "Just wait."

By the time we rolled into the campground, Keilani was leaning out of her window, gaping.

I grinned, taking in the familiar view for myself, as we got our first glimpse of Fruita Campground, nestled in a desert farming valley, ringed by red rock cliffs hundreds of feet high. Rustic log fences surrounded pale grass-green campsites, mottled with bright red patches of desert soil peeping through. Spreading shade trees waited for our hammocks.

"I love this place," Mom sighed. "No cell phone coverage. No clients."

"No ABC plan?" I laughed.

"Ha. There's always a plan!" She pointed to the mountain of gear in the back. "How do you think all the food and bedding and first aid supplies got here? You want to sleep on rocks? Kill a lizard for dinner?"

"Okay, okay."

"Don't knock the plan, is all I'm saying. Without my plan, this place is just a dry, crusty, inhospitable desert."

"Hey!" Dad backed the van over the grumbling gravel parking pad. "You're a dry, crusty, inhospitable desert." He grinned at her as he parked the car.

Mom's expressive eyebrows had some things to say in that moment, let me tell you.

He just laughed and planted a kiss on her forehead.

"Eew," I said.

"Eeeew," Budge agreed.

"It's *not* gross when Mom and Dad kiss," Janie said. "I grew out of thinking that. I think it's nice."

"Thank you very much, Janie." Mom planted one on Dad for real.

"Oh, boy. Everybody out. Now." I shoved open my door, and we spilled out into the golden sunshine.

Usually it was funny when Mom and Dad were like this, but not in front of Keilani. Not with her parents splitting up.

Dad stretched, taking in the view. "Should we hike first? Leave setup 'til later?"

"Ha," Mom said. "Your idea of a good time is being so far out in the wilderness that no one would find your corpse if you fell and died while squirming over a giant rock. But the rest of us need an oasis. Hammocks and tents first."

He shrugged. "Okay, kiddos. Head to the amphitheater."

"While Mom and Dad set up camp, we always use the stage where the rangers do their nighttime presentations to perform wild theatricals," I told Keilani. "That way our neighbor-campers don't know how super annoying we are right at first." I leaned in close to whisper, "Also so we don't have to help with camp setup. It's a win-win."

"I heard that," Mom said, hauling out camp chairs.

I framed my chin with my hands, beaming an innocent smile. She rolled her eyes, but she was smiling too.

I loved that I could still get away with slacking off sometimes.

"What neighbor-campers?" Keilani gestured to the sites around us, filled with still, silent motor homes. The only people in sight were a couple eating sandwiches over a checkered tablecloth and a white-haired man, snoozing in a hammock.

"This," Mom said, "is why we come to Capitol Reef, not Zion or Arches. You can breathe and think here. But others want that peace too, and my children are . . . How do I put this delicately?"

"A Noise-pocalypse?" Keilani laughed.

"Exactly." Mom double-tapped her nose. "Please take the Noise-pocalypse somewhere else."

"Get out of here," Dad huffed under the weight of our massive canvas tent, and Mom hurried to grab one side. "We got this."

"Hope you're in the singing and dancing mood." I made jazz hands at Keilani. "It's showtime."

"I won't say no to a little singing and dancing," she said. "But you should have invited Hrishi instead of me if you wanted an epic performance. At least according to him." She rolled her eyes, but she was also smiling like she could already picture him strutting around the stage.

"You'll be amazing," I assured her. "But yeah. Most things are more fun with Hrishi."

"Don't tell him that." She gave me a knowing look. "His head's already swollen as it is."

By the time we had Budge's shoes back on, Janie's "Hiking Survival Backpack" that she insisted on carrying everywhere, and sunblock on every face, Mom and Dad were having their annual play-argument about where to put the tent.

"Shaaade," Mom said. "For my naaaps."

"The shady spots are all dirt. Which will be mud if it rains."

"It won't rain. It's why I always schedule this for June—the month with the lowest rainfall."

"You'll nap in your rainbow hammock anyway," he said.

"Maybe, but your precious tent will survive contact with a little dirt."

He shook his head. "Got to protect our investment. This tent will last a lifetime if we treat it right."

"*I'll* last a lifetime if you treat me right," Mom laughed.

He hooked an arm around her waist, pulling her close.

Mom did always say Capitol Reef was where she discovered she was in love with Dad. Hiking Sulphur Creek together, right after she crossed the second waterfall.

"Gross," I muttered. My parents could be so embarrassing. "Let's go."

"Not gross." Keilani took Budge by one hand, and Janie by the other. "I need your parents in my life. They help me believe in forever."

Chapter 11

AFTER

*F*orever is a good word to describe the drive to Capitol Reef with Budge and Janie squirming and arguing and kicking the back of my seat. It's a relief when the brown and white "Welcome to Capitol Reef" sign finally comes into focus—I'm about one kick away from launching into the back seat and throttling them.

I slide my hands over the reassuringly smooth paper of my master plan lying in my lap. I spent every free minute on Friday perfecting it, even including backup plans for bad weather or Budge meltdowns. The full plan is on the app, but without cell service, I want it solidly here where I can hold on to it.

It's not my original get-ready-for-school plan, but Dad's right. Plans should be flexible. That's the whole point of Mom's system.

I'm still thinking of swapping Monday and Thursday's hikes in case our muscles are sore after Sulphur Creek, but I need to stop obsessing.

I shake my hands like I'm physically releasing the anxiety—another Alejandro strategy. A reset signal to my brain.

This plan is as perfect as I can make it.

It's just . . .

I need our first camping trip without Mom to succeed so

everyone will get along and no one will melt down—especially me—and Dad will still trust me to plan for us when we get home, and not even think about moving us away.

No pressure.

We drive into the campground, ringed by soaring rock cliffs, past the weathered pioneer barn and the faded stucco Gifford Farmhouse, where we buy homemade ice cream. The horses munch fallen fruit under the pear tree by the fence. The same horses. The same fruit. Well, not the same actual fruit because four seasons and decomposition and the circle of life and everything.

I guess I thought this place would look different, like the Plan B version of its old Plan A self. But it's the same old Capitol Reef—our home away from home.

We pull up to our campsite. The same exact site as every other year.

My heart pounds hard in my chest, and I don't want to get out of the car.

"Okay," Dad says brightly. "Let's do this."

He hops out to start unloading.

I step out of the van, clutching my plan. The warm breeze brushes my face, stirs my hair.

You love this place. You'll be happy together here.

The thought is a tentative brush against my mind, and a shiver washes over me, in spite of the August heat.

It's like right after she died, when I could almost see her, almost hear her.

The last time we were in Capitol Reef, she was here loving it with us. All it takes is that hint of her voice, and suddenly the orchards, and cliffs, and sun-faded sky are full of her.

I planned safe, but exhilarating hikes. I planned delicious camping meals. I planned stargazing and deer watching.

I don't have a plan for this.

I'm still standing by the van, staring into space, when Janie and Budge start dragging me toward the amphitheater.

I consult my printout. "No. We're helping Dad set up. It's not a one-person job." Those words burn in my throat.

"Aww!" they whine together.

"It's fine. I can handle it." Dad hefts our giant tent, staggering toward the campsite.

"Come on!" Janie begs. "Remember last year when Keilani did 'Let It Go' and we were the ice crystals freezing everything?"

It's hard to believe that was only a year ago. Keilani didn't stop her off-key belting, even when those two teenage boys stopped in the orchard to watch.

I can't imagine her *letting it go* quite so easily now that Mackelle—the ultimate authority on how *not* to embarrass yourself in junior high—is her shadow.

"This year can we do *Tangled*? I'll be Rapunzel, and you and Budgie can be my hair?"

"Um . . . weird . . . And still no." I can't be dragged off plan this soon.

"But—"

"*But*, I've got special jobs for you."

"Special?" Janie folds her stubborn arms.

"Top secret and something only you can help with." I bend to whisper in her ear. "With your artistic skills, I need you to be the camp designer."

She raises a Mom-worthy skeptical eyebrow.

"No, really. You'll find the perfect place for each hammock and chair. And arrange the whole inside of the tent. Dad and I are lost without you, see?" I point across the campsite, where Dad stands by himself, as out of place as a lone pine in a meadow, scanning the hard earth for a tent spot.

"Well . . ." She taps her lip with her pointer finger. "I do think the camp chairs would be best over here in a circle around the fire pit. In rainbow color order, maybe."

"Exactly!"

That's all it takes to get Janie moving. But I'm still watching Dad, who seems unsure for the first time in his life about where he wants the tent to go.

I bite down hard on my lower lip. Mom is too real here.

His shoulders slump, then he blinks quickly and walks straight to a shady site with patchy grass. It's like he let Mom win their argument, even though she's not here.

I don't want to think about her every time I climb into our shady tent, and I'm about to suggest a sunny spot, but a crash from the van makes me spin around. Budge stands guiltily beside an upended tub of kitchen supplies.

"Hey!" I rush over to him.

"I was helping." He stamps his foot. "You said we got fun

jobs, but Janie won't let me move the chairs and you're not even helping, so why can't we go to the amphitheater, 'cause I'm booored."

"I saved you the best job of all," I say, scooping pots and scrubbies out of the dirt and back into the tub, hoping the perfect idea will fall from the sky and hit me on the head. Most of the camping gear is too heavy for Budge, and I obviously can't leave him alone.

"You're my personal assistant," I announce with a sigh. At least this way I can keep track of him.

But I trip over him every time I carry a load from the van. And his main contribution is messing up my organizational system, unpacking tubs one paper towel roll and Sharpie at a time. I can't lose those. I need them to label baggies when we pack lunch for our first hike.

"Wait! I've got a better job for you!"

"Whaaat?" Budge bounces on his toes.

"Protector of the Camping Plan!" I say the words like I'm proclaiming him Grand Ruler of all Capitol Reef. "Sit in your camp chair and guard the plan until Dad gets the first hammock set up. Then you can swing in the hammock and keep our plan safe from dirt and bugs."

This powerful new title and the promise of first hammock turn keep Budge uncharacteristically patient and quiet, while complete artistic control over camp furniture keeps Janie smug and productive.

We set up camp quicker than I thought possible, and the kitchen organization looks almost as good as Mom's.

Dad starts stringing hammocks in the spots Janie selected, and soon the rainbow hammock he gave Mom a few Christmases ago sways in the breeze like it's waiting for her to bring her book and trail mix.

I look quickly away.

Budge gleefully abandons his camp chair. "Help me up!" He tries unsuccessfully to launch himself into the hammock.

"Good job, Budge. You were so patient." I laugh at his flailing attempts. "Here, let me help y—"

My mouth falls open in horror.

"Budge!"

In place of my smooth, neatly organized camping plan, his chubby, grubby hands clutch a crinkled wad of paper. It's smeared with red Capitol Reef dirt and written all over in thick black marker.

I thought I had gathered the Sharpies, but apparently Budge held on to one. He has used my camping plan as one of his notebooks—from the looks of things, his first full-novel attempt.

My perfect plan is completely unreadable.

Chapter 12

BEFORE

"Who *doesn't* make plans for the future?" Mackelle said in her who-*doesn't*-wash-their-hands-after-going-to-the-bathroom voice. She reclined in my mom's zero gravity patio chair and straightened her stack of papers for Mansion, Apartment, Shack, House, or M.A.S.H.

Telling fortunes with M.A.S.H. was a current primary focus of sixth-grade girls, and one of the only socially acceptable recess activities for the lip-gloss crowd—where I still thought Mackelle belonged.

"I make plans." I folded my arms across my chest. "M.A.S.H. isn't a plan. It's a silly counting game that means nothing."

"If it means nothing, why not do it?" Keilani shrugged. "Spring soccer games start next week, and then we'll be busy every Saturday. This is fun."

Fun? Mackelle must be rubbing off on her.

I was probably being a jerk, because new girl with no other friends, and blah, blah, blah. But if Keilani hadn't insisted on inviting her over, we could be playing killer Uno with Hrishi. Or having a sing-off on the retired karaoke setup the Patels let us mess around with—at least until Mrs. Patel kicked us out for Mama's Silent Reading Time.

Or just . . . you know . . . *not* hanging out with Mackelle.

Yup. Definitely being a jerk. I sighed. I wish I could be annoyed by her without feeling guilty about it too.

I slipped off my plastic chair to flop down in the grass, cool in the spring sunshine, and carefully removed any attitude from my voice. "All right. Tell my future."

"Keilani first." Mackelle rubbed her glossy lips together, clicking her pen dramatically. "I already started on her before I got here."

Fine with me.

"Keilani," Mackelle placed her pen deliberately on the M.A.S.H. form. "Tell me one car, one job, one—"

"Doesn't she need like four or five of each?" I might have thought M.A.S.H. was useless, but it wasn't like I'd been homeschooled for the last two months.

"It's better if the person telling your future provides all but one option in each category."

"Really?" Keilani sat up straighter, trying to peek over Mackelle's shoulder at her future options for car, job, number of children, only dinner option for all time, best friend, and soul mate.

Mackelle swiped the papers away, waggling her finger at Keilani. "You can't see. If you repeat one I already have for you, we leave it in twice. It's the universe's way of giving your desired destiny a little help. Car?"

"Hot tub Hummer," Keilani said. "Easy."

"Job."

"Team USA soccer coach."

"Yes!" I reached up from my grass lounger to fist bump for Team USA.

"One and only meal."

"Orange chicken."

"Love interest."

Keilani groaned, proving she hadn't had her brain replaced by aliens. "Thor," she said.

"Nope. Rules specifically state it has to be someone you really know."

Which rules? The rules of being a sixth-grade girl, or the rules of Mackelle being the boss of the world?

"Someone you really know," she repeated. "And, like, probably someone that wouldn't make you barf if you had to kiss them someday."

I could feel my nose wrinkling like Mackelle's had earlier, and Keilani had patches of red creeping up her neck.

"That doesn't really describe anyone," Keilani said. "All the boys we know are in the sixth grade."

Fair point. Sixth-grade boys were . . . I shuddered.

"Just put Hrishi," I said quickly. "He's the only boy we know who's consistently not gross."

Keilani shrugged. "Uh, okay. Put Hrishi, I guess. He is not disgusting."

"How romantic!" Mackelle giggled. "He'd die and go to heaven if he knew you thought he was, 'not disgusting.'"

Keilani rolled her eyes.

"Best friend?" Mackelle asked.

"Morgan," Keilani said without hesitation.

I shot her a grin.

"Gee, thanks." Mackelle blew out a mock-annoyed puff of air.

"Oh, sorry," said Keilani, flustered. "I didn't mean . . . do you already have Morgan on there?"

"Of course."

"Okay, um . . . definitely put you then."

"Yay!" Mackelle wrote her name with a flourish. "I already added myself. Which means you've got twice as many chances of landing me as your best friend forever."

I gave Keilani a looook, but her return look spoke actual words: *Give her a chance. She needs us. She's new here.*

Hmph.

Mackelle picked unlucky 13 as the magic prediction number. (Of course she did.) Then she pulled out her Sharpie to cross out the eliminated options and turned to screen the M.A.S.H. from our view while she foretold Keilani's doom . . . ahem . . . future. She kept shaking her head or squealing with glee every time she crossed something off.

"No soup for you." Giggle. Giggle. "Ooh. No limo either." She clucked her tongue regretfully. "Ooh, sad. You will not be coaching Team USA. But! You will also not be marrying Sam Kluggur."

I gave a low whistle. Mackelle was out for blood. Sam was a notorious nose-picker. Still. In the sixth grade.

"Sam!" Keilani shouted loud enough that if Mrs. Patel was having Silent Reading Time, we were in for it. Hrishi's mom took books very seriously. "Show me that list," she demanded.

"Don't worry," Mackelle said. "You've still got Hrishi on there, twice."

"Hrishi on where, twice?" said a loud voice.

All three of us jumped. The voice was Hrishi's. And so was the head, laughing at us over our side fence, his hair sticking up in every direction even more than usual. His comb must've taken the weekend off. "Heard my name, so I came, even if you all *didn't* invite me to this party."

I laughed back at him. "You know you don't need an invitation."

"Yes," he grunted as he hoisted himself over the fence, landing lightly on my back lawn. "I do know that." He beamed, white teeth bright in his golden-brown face, dimples popping out. "I'm your favorite." He kicked my bare toes. Lightly, since he was wearing running shoes. "But where is my name? And why twice?"

"We were just predicting Kei—"

"On the . . . um . . . invitations to our *next* party." Keilani snatched the clipboard and Sharpie from Mackelle, and started writing furiously. "So you wouldn't feel bad about today." She laughed, but it had a sharp, tight sound to it. "You're invited twice."

Seriously? I got why she didn't want to talk bra-shopping

with Hrishi, but this? Hrishi would just ask why his name wasn't on there five times. Or demand his future be told next. What was her deal?

When she held up the paper for Hrishi to see, the whole M.A.S.H. was covered in thick black Sharpie letters. Completely unreadable.

GUESTS

FOR

PARTY:

US

HRISHI PATEL

HRISHI PATEL

Then she giggled. A totally un-Keilani noise.

Seriously? I should tell her to wipe off that Mackelle she's got all over her.

"What have you done?" Mackelle squealed. "You'll be cursed. And probably your children too. What kind of future can you hope for when you've desecrated a M.A.S.H.? If you end up marrying Sam, don't blame me."

The image of Keilani and Sam raising piles of little nose-picking kids together made me laugh. But Keilani was too busy blasting Mackelle with her "shut up" stare to join me.

"What's going *on* with you guys?" Hrishi cocked his head at us.

"Nothing," Mackelle and Keilani said together, then Mackelle got the giggles again.

"Morgan?" Hrishi's baffled eyebrows practically met in the middle.

I shrugged.

I wasn't entirely sure.

Sensible, mellow Keilani was acting like Mackelle—all silly around boys. Even worse? She was acting like Hrishi was a *boy*. Hrishi Patel—a *boy*.

But this was twice now—Keilani acting like her big sister Tama's giggly friends, who were all about celebrity influencers on Insta and YouTube makeup tutorials—girls we used to make fun of.

With Mackelle hanging around more and more, the Hrishi-Morgan-Keilani triangle was morphing into a squashed, off-kilter quadrilateral—a trapezoid.

Or was that a rhombus? Geometry was hardly my favorite part of school.

"Uh . . . should I go?" Both of Hrishi's eyebrows were about to meet his messy hairline.

"Yeah." I scrambled to my feet. "And I'll go with you."

"Yes!" He did a double fist pump. "*Clone Wars*! We're almost to the Umbara arc, when you'll finally understand how awesome Rex and Fives are, and you'll be begging *me* for more episodes. But just remember this arc is way depressing, so when you turn to a puddle of tears, don't say I didn't warn you!"

I looked to Keilani for commiseration. While we both liked Star Wars, neither of us saw our future as Hrishi's Jedi Padawans.

But Keilani just stared down at her marker-massacred-M.A.S.H. No solidarity coming my way.

"Whatever." I shrugged at Hrishi, heading for the gate like a normal person while he vaulted over the fence like . . . well . . . like himself. "I'm in as long as it's not another Jar Jar episode."

Clone Wars or no *Clone Wars*, at least over at Hrishi's, I still understood geometry.

Chapter 13

AFTER

"Budge! You had one job! How am I supposed to—Dad!" I wave the destroyed plan at him.

"What's going on?"

"My plan!" I put a hand over my chest, feel my heart pounding through my shirt.

Dad pats my shoulder like I'm Janie, freaking out after Budge ate the last cherry sucker. I pull away.

"It's going to be okay," he says brightly.

"But the menus. If we eat the wrong things, we won't have what we need for other meals and—"

"It's just food. We'll work with what we've got." His voice tries and fails to soothe me.

"And the schedule! I planned *everything*."

"Let's just go hiking. We've got this, I promise."

It will not just "be okay." Budge destroying my plan feels like a sign of things to come.

And not a good sign. More like when Hrishi's favorite Jedi are always *sensing* that the Force is super disturbed.

I'm tired of acting mature and holding it together. I want to throw the cherry sucker tantrum of the century. I want to yell at my five-year-old brother for two or three hours, then collapse in a hammock and cry my eyes out. But I need Dad to know *I've* got this.

I clamp my teeth shut, breathe in through my nose for a count of four, hold for four, and breathe out for eight.

Not sure why the counting matters, but Alejandro says it does. So while Dad preps for an afternoon hike to Who Knows Where by throwing bagels and yogurt tubes into his pack, I'm all: *breathe, two, three, four.*

Pretty sure those bagels and yogurt were tomorrow's breakfast.

Hold, two, three, four.

I'd know if I'd organized like Mom. She always laminated the menu onto the food bin, which of course I forgot to do.

Out, two, three, four, five, six, seven, eight.

I'd also know if Budge hadn't covered my plan with tips for winning at *Mario Kart.* At least I think that's what he meant when he wrote SHOOT THE RED SHEL AT THER BUTS.

Dad puts an arm around my shoulders. "You okay, kiddo?"

I nod.

"You should use this trip to relax," he says soothingly. "You've worked so hard this summer."

My eyes burn, and I pull away. I learned pretty quick after Mom died that sympathy from anyone else makes it harder for me to keep it together.

"Come on," Dad says. "We're together in this awesome place. You don't plan for perfection like this."

I open my mouth to say that Mom always did. That none of us is ready for the chaos if I take his advice.

Instead, I press my lips into a thin line, try to stretch them into a smile. I can't talk about Mom. It wouldn't come out in a gentle trickle. It's a roaring, flooding river. And my only safe option is keeping it all inside.

Chapter 14
AFTER

Capitol Gorge is spectacular. I mean, the trail is just a wash—a dried-up riverbed made of rock and sand that only wishes it still flowed with water. But on either side of us, Swiss cheese canyon walls, riddled with waterworn caves and holes of all sizes, rise out of the red, dusty ground. It's nature's very own jungle gym—for Budge and Janie.

But with Budge climbing into every last crevice, Dad and Janie are almost around the next bend in the canyon.

"Take my picture!" Budge is curled up, filling a barely-boy-sized pocket in the canyon wall. His eyes are nearly closed, lips stretched wide and thin in his awkward five-year-old camera smile.

"Okay, but no more climbing. We need to catch up." I snap the pic, but before I can put the phone safely away, Budge worms out of the hole.

"Wait!" I lunge forward, barely getting a hand under him in time to slow his slide to the sandy ground. It's like he wants to get hurt.

"Heeeyyy, I was wall-jumping. Didn't you know I can wall-jump?"

Suddenly I know how to hurry him along.

"But there's lava in this level. We have to race, or it'll catch us."

Just like that, his chubby legs propel him at a sprint over the rocky wash floor. But as we round the bend in the trail, I see nothing but narrow canyon walls and flat sandy floor.

"Dad!"

The word echoes back, taunting. They can't have gotten far.

"Janie!" I call. Which is when I hear giggling, high above us.

Halfway up the canyon wall to the right, Dad and Janie hide in a giant hole—Siblings' Cave.

It was Morgan's cave until Janie first joined me inside and it became Sisters' Cave. A couple of years later, we expanded the name to fit Budge. With all the climbing, I didn't think we'd come this far.

Even though we've grown, it's still large enough to hold our whole family. Although Mom never made that climb. She said watching us go so high made her teeth itch. The last couple of years I ran up without help, but today the rock face looks impossibly steep.

"Come up, guys!" Janie leans out of the cave far enough to make *me* feel dizzy.

"Careful, Janie! Dad, grab her."

"She's fine. Come on up. I've got a surprise activity."

Budge is already trying to launch up the slick rock, but with no handholds, he slides back down.

"Help him, Morgan."

I'm frozen in place. Siblings' Cave is the highlight of the hike, but the canyon walls feel too tall and too close together, squeezing in on me. It might have felt safe before, when Mom did the worrying for me. But today?

I am not helping a five-year-old climb that canyon wall.

"I can do it myself!" Budge throws himself at the wall again and again, trying different angles. "It's like getting a star coin. There's always a solution. You just have to look at it a different way."

I roll my eyes. It's what he always says about video games.

Dad starts down toward us, pointing his toes carefully toward the canyon floor like he taught us, to grip the rock better. "Come on. Help Budge-Man reach me."

I sigh.

Budge is probably in more danger trying to climb on his own, so I hold the soles of his sneakers against the smooth sandstone like Dad always did for me, helping him get a grip in more ways than one.

Once they reach the nearly invisible seam that we use as a pathway to the cave, Budge runs up by himself, and Dad comes back for me.

I fold my arms tightly around myself. "It's dangerous. You should bring the kids down."

He chuckles at that. "*The kids* are safe," he says. "I'm all over it—taking good care of them. And you too. Come on."

I shake my head. My legs feel like Jell-O.

I'm with you, girl. Keeping both feet on the ground is always my Plan A.

I gasp. Mom's voice in my head is so real I whip my head around.

She's not there, of course. But for a second I can almost see her out of the corner of my eye, her ponytail dangling under her wide-brimmed hiking hat, hands in the back pockets of her cargo shorts.

This climb is bonkers. Mom's voice—if only in my mind—saying what she always said when we climbed to Siblings' Cave.

I always thought if she tried, she'd see it's not that bad. Today I'm seeing things from her perspective—feeling her fear of heights for her.

Not heights. Falling, Almost-Mom says. *High things are fine, as long as there's no danger of me or anyone I love falling off them.*

I don't want her in my head this whole trip.

"Come on, Morgan." Dad's voice is bright as he holds out his hand.

Let her be, Josh. It's her choice.

Ha.

It's exactly what Real Mom would say. Dad's relentless once he has an idea, and even if I wish she weren't talking in my head, I can borrow her words.

"It's my choice," I say. "I'm not climbing today."

Dad gives me a sharp look, like he heard her, or at least heard her in me.

He nods finally. "Okay. If you want, you can participate from down there."

Like Mom always did.

I scuff my feet back and forth, stirring the sand of the canyon floor. I've got a sudden need to run until I'm breathless and kick the air out of a soccer ball.

"Lunch." Dad walks back down the steep canyon wall to hand me a bagel and a yogurt tube.

I walk across the canyon, where shade pools on a flat slab of sandstone, and sit, resting my back. I wash lunch down with slurps of cool water from my hydration pack, enjoying the quiet of everyone eating.

It doesn't last long.

"You guys want dessert?" Dad says brightly.

"Yay!" Janie yells.

"All right! Today's dessert . . ." Dad pauses like he's waiting for a drum roll. "Is also the surprise activity."

He reaches into his backpack and pulls out a bundle, wrapped in one of his camping tee shirts.

He unveils an all-too-familiar blue willow crock, and opens it up, setting the lid on the sandstone ledge next to him. Like it's totally normal to bring fine porcelain and one of Mom's most prized possessions out on a hike where one move from Budge could send it tumbling to its doom.

But that's not what keeps my objections stuck tight in my throat.

The crock is full to the brim with—

"Lemon drops!" Janie shrieks in delight.

My bagel turns to solid rock in my stomach. How did he find them? I hid them so carefully behind the—Oh. Behind the camping dishes.

Dad watches me from above like he can read my mind.

I can already taste the sour.

"Yup. Lemon drops. Dessert *and* an activity." He says the words in a voice all bright and hopeful, but his anxious expression doesn't match his tone.

Budge and Janie cheer, oblivious.

I stare down at my worn-out running shoes in the red canyon dirt. The canister of lemon drops feels like Mom's rainbow hammock times ten.

"Since this is a trip we loved to do with Mom, I thought we'd each have a lemon drop a couple times a day, take time to talk about her, remember her."

My eyes sting, and I blink quickly, glad Dad's not close enough to see.

I remember her plenty. If Dad knew how much, he'd worry more than he already does.

It's okay, Morgan. Almost-Mom's voice is a whisper. *You can do this.*

Is it normal to hear your dead mom's voice in your head? To feel her with you so strong, the real world fades in comparison?

"Everyone take a lemon drop, and I'll ask a question we can talk about."

"That's not how lemon drops work," I mutter.

"What?" Dad calls down.

"You don't give someone a lemon drop. They ask when they need one." Most of the time. Even Mom offered lemon drops when she thought we needed them. But I'm not letting that stop me. "Also, you don't tell people what to talk about. The whole point of a lemon drop is talking about *what* you want, *when* you want." I press my back against the rough, cool stone behind me.

"I want one!" Janie squeals.

"Me too!" Budge nods his curly blond head super-fast.

Dad passes them both a drop. Clearly, no one else cares that we're doing this all wrong.

"No one has to have a lemon drop unless they want one," Dad says carefully. "But for this first drop, let's share one thing we remember about Mom from other camping trips."

"Snuggling in our sleeping bags!" Budge shouts, launching to his feet. "Mom says snuggling is one of my talents."

"She's correct, Budge-Man." Dad gives him a squeeze.

"Playing I Spy on our hikes," Janie says. "Mom can always . . . um . . . Mom *could* always spy really interesting things."

Dad nods. Looks up at the sky while he pats Janie on the shoulder awkwardly. I wait for The Fog to roll in, split us safely apart.

I'm pretty sure the word that's hurting him is the same one that's making me hold my breath.

Could.

It's the exact reason this lemon drop idea is my nemesis. We *could* have lemon drops. They *could* help. That was before.

"Morgan?" Dad stands, ready to walk my "dessert" down to me. "You can talk about something different if you want to. Anything really."

But answers to his lemon drop question flood my mind: Hammocks. Climbing anxiety. Perfect plans that no one destroys.

"No, thanks." I keep my expression neutral.

"You sure?" He watches me with eyes so clear of The Fog that I have to look down at my feet instead of up at him while I nod.

I'm definitely sure. I'm not having a lemon drop. Dad wants me to talk about my feelings, but he has no idea what he's asking for.

Chapter 15

BEFORE

Our van was like a funeral the whole drive home after our loss to the Warriors. We were probably being rude, but Mom kept trying to get Brianna, Keilani, Fishy Mackelle, and me to chat. She even offered consolation ice cream, but we all just wanted to make it home without crying in front of each other.

The week before, we'd beaten Rocky Mountain—the biggest question mark on our schedule—stealing their first-place ranking.

Our match against the Warriors today should have just padded our score and brought us closer to home field advantage when we hit tournament at the end of April.

But we lost, one–nothing.

In overtime.

Against *the Warriors.*

The week before, Rocky Mountain had destroyed them—a mercy roll after the score hit 9–1 in the first half.

"Mercy roll" is soccer-speak for "end early to put them out of their misery."

We should have destroyed them.

Brianna was sniffling in the back seat. As keeper, I'm pretty sure she thought the game-losing goal was her fault.

"You'll have better luck next time," Mom said.

Silence.

"I'm so proud of you."

Silence.

"I mean it. All of you. You played your hearts out."

"It was Soccer-pocalypse, Mama Bell," Keilani said.

She wasn't wrong. But Mom wasn't giving up that easily.

"You all had great plays. And you, Brianna—so many great saves."

Sniff. "Thanks, Ms. Bell."

"And Mackelle. What a shot, right there at the end."

Mackelle tossed her high ponytail. Keilani had her hair in a high pony too—first time I'd seen her play without her signature braids.

"Thanks, Mama Bell." Mackelle's words raised the hair on the back of my neck. She didn't know Mom well enough for *Mama Bell.*

Who did she think she was? Keilani 2.0?

And sure, she had one great shot. When Coach subbed her in for me after my *eight* shots.

She wasn't Morgan 2.0 either.

Mom drove in silence while we stared out the windows.

Then suddenly—*screeeech.*

I slid sideways, smooshing into the passenger door as Mom swerved the van in a 360—tight and fast, like a sports car.

All four of us squealed.

"Mom, what—"

"Hold on tight, girls!" she said. "Plan A was celebration ice cream. Plan B? Consolation ice cream. Well, text your parents, because it's time for Plan C—cleaning up these attitudes. I thought I was driving home the Blue Thunder, but I'm not spending another minute with the Blue Thunderclouds. Text your whole team. Morgan, give them the Patels' address." She handed me her phone.

"You want me to send the team to Hrishi's house?" She wasn't making any sense.

"No, the restaurant." Mom laughed. "Then call and warn Fariq and Jesminder to prepare for a crowd."

My eyes were wide as I dialed Hrishi's family's restaurant and karaoke bar.

You didn't argue with Mom when she hit Plan C.

Two hours of karaoke and four savory platters of samosas later—all of us laughing as Keilani belted out "Fight Song" in an off-key country twang—no one much cared about the Warriors and their suddenly superpowered goalie.

Mom had sung first to break the ice—a hilariously shrill oldie. At which point Mackelle put on her surprised face and mouthed, "Your mom's cool."

That's right, Mackelle. And you thought you knew her well enough to call her Mama Bell?

Hrishi's parents had called him and his older brother Kiaan in to help serve when they heard we were coming, but they weren't much help, other than livening up the party. They took the stage together to belt out "I Wanna Hold Your Hand," in practiced harmony, while Kiaan strutted around, reaching out like he wanted to hold hands with every girl on my soccer team. (Brianna and Mackelle took him up on it. Repeatedly.) Hrishi kept motioning for me to join them as backup, but I was laughing too hard.

Mackelle's mouth was going again, this time to overemphasize the words, "They're a-DOR-able."

Brianna squealed, "I know, right?"

I rolled my eyes at them. It was just Hrishi and Kiaan.

Halfway through Mackelle and Keilani's off-key rendition of "Girls Just Wanna Have Fun," Hrishi slipped into a chair at my table. He grinned, sliding over a plate of my favorite gulab jamun, still warm, and drizzled with extra rose syrup. His hair stuck up on top like he'd just climbed out of bed.

"Sorry you guys lost." He stretched his feet under the table to kick my toes in commiseration.

"And to *the Warriors*." I double-toe-tapped him back. "Yeah. It was the worst."

He tilted his face to the side, twisting up his mouth in sympathy.

"But *these* are not the worst." I punched him in the arm for thanks and popped one of the fried cakes into my mouth, letting the sweet syrup coat my tongue.

"You want to sing with me?" Hrishi looked up and away from me like he didn't want to hear my answer.

"Duh," I said.

Dimples appeared in both his cheeks.

Not sure why he asked. We always sang together.

All the parents came to the restaurant to collect their kids, so on the way home it was just Mom and me.

I relaxed back in my seat, fingers drumming the rhythm of that One Direction song Hrishi and I sang while Brianna, Keilani, and Mackelle waved their cell phones like it was a real concert.

"How do you do that?" I turned to look at Mom. She looked beautiful, even in an old tee shirt, with her hair slipping out of her ponytail.

"Do what?" She shook her head, confused.

"Make everything all better."

She laughed, reaching over to squeeze my shoulder. "I'm a mom, Morgan. It's in the job description."

Chapter 16
AFTER

Janie wakes up crying in the night. Her sobs fill the tent, my heart, and possibly the whole campground. A nightmare or something, and when she wakes up, there's no Mom, waiting to do her job and make it all better.

Dad does his best, but it takes him a long time to comfort her. I lie still, pretending to be asleep. I'm pretty sure he doesn't notice I'm awake, even though he doesn't go back to sleep either. I can tell from his breathing.

Janie's so peppy all the time that I sometimes wonder if she even misses Mom. But maybe she only lets herself feel it at night in her dreams—when she can't hold it back anymore.

In the morning, her eyes are red, her whole face pinched together around the edges. Budge is a rage-beast, yelling at everyone that he lost his notebook and he needs to write words RIGHT NOW.

Be brave for them. Help them be happy.

It doesn't take me long to find Budge's notebook under his sleeping pad. The bigger challenge is Janie, sitting listless in her camp chair, staring at the dead coals from last night's fire.

I should focus on what I can control—The Plan.

We stopped by the visitor center yesterday after our hike to use their Wi-Fi to sync my plan to Mom's phone. I also tweaked the schedule and menus to make up for the Budge-Plan-Destruction detour. The updated plan is stored safely on the phone in my pocket, and Dad promised we can follow it today—for the schedule at least.

He still wants to sprinkle lemon drops all through this vacation.

Lemon Drop #2 (last night after dinner): *What's a gift Mom gave you that you really appreciated?*

Budge: *Smash Bros. Brawl*

Janie: *My Hiking Survival Backpack with all the supplies.*

Dad: *You three.*

Me: *Lots of things. I can't pick just one. We should clean up and get to bed. Early day tomorrow.*

"Instant oatmeal this morning?" Dad sets the pot on the stove.

He's right. I already checked the menu. But it's Janie's least favorite breakfast.

I grimace. "I don't think we're in a very oatmeal mood."

"Oatmeal is the food of hiking champions," Dad says. "Backpacking the Great Western Trail I ate it every day for—"

"Sixty days straight," I finish. "I know. But plans have to be flexible, right? Could you prep backpacks for Cohab Canyon? I'll take Janie and Budge to buy Gifford Farmhouse pie for breakfast. My treat. I've got allowance money."

"Morgan is the best sister in the wooorld!" Budge shouts.

A man in the next campsite looks up sharply from his coffee cup, like he's trying to remind us it's still early. But I don't care—Janie has a half smile playing about her lips.

Hurrah for flexible plans! We'll eat oatmeal tomorrow.

"Morgan *is* the best." Dad's words warm me, even though full sunlight hasn't hit the valley yet. "But you don't need to spend your money. I've got it." He heads to the car for his wallet.

"No, I want to." This treat should be mine. I'm just keeping my promise.

He hesitates for a moment, then smiles, gives me a quick nod. "I'll get our packs ready. Beautiful day for my favorite hike."

"Every hike is your favorite hike." I roll my eyes.

"It *looks* like a beautiful day, but it's going to rain." Janie squints up at the sky. "See how those clouds are all puffy? We learned cloud types in the water cycle unit. Those aren't cumulus or cirrus. See how tall and dark those are? They're cu-mu-lo-nim-bus."

"You're cumulonimbus." Dad pulls our packs from the van.

"It's not going to rain." I eye the clouds gathering over Cohab Canyon with my sternest expression. "I checked last night at the visitor center. The ranger with the long curly hair said most likely not."

Dad shakes his head. "No. He said, 'I dunno, dude. Twenty

percent chance means probably not. But around here, dude? Anything can happen. *Anything.*'"

Janie's smile turns smug. "Wait and see," she says. "Cumulonimbus clouds mean rain."

"Agree to disagree," I say. My sixth-grade teacher Mr. Morton always said that when people argued. I like it. It means I can be right, while the other person thinks whatever they want.

By the time we arrive at Gifford Farmhouse, Janie and Budge are arguing over peach or apple.

"How do you feel about cherry?" I ask.

Barfing noises. That's how they feel about cherry.

Gifford Farmhouse had better have peach or apple in stock.

But the plump, aproned woman at the counter shakes her head apologetically, pointing at the empty glass pie case. "There's a family reunion at the group site with twenty-five very hungry grandchildren," she explains. "Maybe you'd like an herbed cheesy scone?"

Budge starts crying at the sight of the lumpy orange and white ball, crusted with herbs. It looks like someone tried to make a snowman in fresh-cut grass. Janie blinks up at me, barely containing her horror.

Desperate for an alternative, I dart my eyes over shelves, bearing bottles of bright, spicy salsas and bowls of corn chips—hardly breakfasty options.

"It's okay. We'll think of a—" I stop myself short of actually saying the words, *Plan B.*

No one deserves to eat Plan B for breakfast, especially when their mouth was ready for flaky pastry and sweet golden fruit.

Then I spy a green and white gingham bag, tied with a ribbon and labeled, "Grandma Peggy's Homemade Hearty Buttermilk Pancakes." It sits beside a row of jewel-toned berry syrups.

"You know what's better than pie?" I put all the optimism I can muster into one word. "Pancakes!"

You know what's not better than berry pie?

Burnt pancakes that stick to the bottom of the frying pan because we can't bring our awesome plug-in griddle to the wilderness.

Also, because clearly I am *not* Mom.

I glare down at the ruined remains of breakfast like my searing eyeballs can scour the evidence of my failure from the pan.

"You okay?" Dad puts a hand on my shoulder.

"Fine." I shift away from his touch so I won't explode while I scrape the guts of Grandma Peggy's Totally Crummy and Burnt to a Crisp Pancake Mix into a grocery bag.

"I can have oatmeal ready in a jiffy," he says hopefully.

I pull out my phone to check the time.

"Let's just do apples and granola bars," I say. "We want to start up Cohab Canyon now so we can be up there at the Frying Pan for lunch."

"True," Dad says. "Especially since Janie thinks it's going to rain later."

"It *will* rain later," she corrects. "Cumulonimbus clouds don't lie."

I roll my eyes. "Everybody eat quick." I grab the frying pan and beeline for the communal rinse-water sink by the bathrooms.

Usually if Dad's home, he does the dinner dishes. Even when Mom was alive, that was always his thing. But I need the alone time to calm down.

I wait impatiently for a potbellied man in a tank top—who should know better—to finish brushing his teeth and spitting *into the dishwashing sink! Blech!*

I rinse the sink for a long time before I start washing the pan.

I forgot the scrubby, and I'm not going back to camp until my face cools off. So I'm clawing at crusty pancake residue with my fingernails when the memory hits me: Mom, standing at our kitchen sink as she dumps a vat of inedible soup into the growling garbage disposal and says words I am so not allowed to use.

I choke on a laugh, oddly comforted. She ruined meals too. Her plans didn't always come together perfectly, and that was a super-special and barf-provoking example. Clam chowder was meant to have milk in it, yes. But not eggnog.

It will be all right. We're here in our favorite place. Where even when the hiking is difficult, we're all somehow still happy.

I'm not letting go of this chance to test out my plan because some pancakes betrayed me.

I'll make this camping trip succeed if it kills me.

Chapter 17

BEFORE

"This hike is going to kill me." Keilani paused to wipe away sweat and gasp in air as we climbed the massive stone stairway in the canyon wall. She seemed to be enjoying her first ever camping trip, but the hike to Cassidy Arch was pushing it. "I feel so out of shape," she moaned. "My only comfort is Hrishi would have already curled up and died somewhere way down at the bottom of the trail."

I stifled a smile. I shouldn't be glad this was hard for her too. But she'd beaten me in every wind sprint since we were six, and I'm only human.

"He absolutely would have curled up and died. He'd be all . . . 'Farewell cruel galaxy. Burn my corpse alongside my lightsaber.'"

Keilani snorted. "Are all the hikes like this?" She shielded her eyes with her hand, squinting up at the trail above us.

"No," Mom groaned. "But they'll keep coming two or three a day until one of us kicks the bucket, or we go home."

"Gotta sacrifice for anything worth seeing," Dad said. "When I was young, I hiked ten to twenty miles a day for sixty days straight on the Great Western Trail." He grinned, remembering. "Two weeks of that entirely on my own."

Janie gasped. "All by yourself?"

"That would be so, so, very not fun." Budge shook his head. "I would never, ever go camping for two weeks all by myself. If you sleep out in the forest aaallll night, you could get eaten by a lot of animals and then you would die and then you would be dead."

"That's usually what happens if you die." I grinned at Keilani over his head.

"It sounds like an adventure." Janie bounced along beside Dad.

Dad ruffled Janie's hair. "It *was* an adventure." He closed his eyes for a second, like he was reliving the hike. "But it was more than that. It was a transformative experience."

"A transformative experience." Janie looked up at Dad like *he* was a transformative experience.

"Yup. Any time you do something challenging like that, it makes you see yourself differently, learn what you're capable of. Plus, being alone in all this beauty?" He spread his arms wide to indicate the soaring red-rock walls around us. "I keep thinking someday your mom will go with me on one of those long backpacking trips."

"You keep thinking that." Her voice was breathless from the climb.

"You like hiking." He slipped an arm around her waist. "You love Sulphur Creek."

"That's Sulphur Creek," she said. "The world's only perfect hike."

"I'm tiiired." Budge slumped against a rock. "I don't care about the arch. Can we go back now?"

Mom raised an eyebrow at Dad.

"Come on, Budge-Man," Dad said. "You always finish the hike. One foot in front of the other. The payoff at the end will be worth it."

"Yeah, Budge," Janie said. "There's an arch at the end, and Daddy says we can walk on top. Don't you want to walk on the arch?"

Dad high fived Janie.

"No one is walking on the arch." Mom's voice was dry as the canyon floor.

"We'll see." Dad scooped up Budge, carrying him over the next several rock stairs.

As we worked our way around the rim of the canyon toward the arch, Mom gasped every time Budge or Janie or even Keilani and I walked too close to the edge.

All the gasping was starting to make my legs feel wobbly.

"I remember why I hate this hike," Mom said. "Why we should never do it again."

"Are you kidding? I love this hike!" Keilani's voice echoed off the canyon walls. She'd regained a lot of energy once we weren't doing switchbacks up a cliff.

"Hullooo!" Budge shouted.

"Hulllllooooooooo!" Janie tried to outdo him.

"Bluuue Thunder!" Keilani shouted, and the echoes cheered with her.

"Keilani! Janie! Follow me!" Budge and Janie ran forward along the narrow trail. And Keilani sped along with them, while I hurried to catch up.

"Careful," Mom called.

"Don't hate the hike," Dad said. "We're more than halfway there. Look. There's the arch." He pointed to where we could just see Cassidy Arch peeking up next to the cliff where we'd view it from above.

"That's what I mean." The anger in Mom's voice made me hold back to hear her. "Why do we always have to hike somewhere our children could fall and die?"

I stumbled over a rock, caught myself, then just stood there, legs shaking.

We could die?

"Morgan!" Keilani called back to me. "Hurry up, or Coach will make you run extra."

I tried to laugh at her joke. But my "Ha! Ha!" fell flat. I glanced back at Mom and Dad.

"No one's dying, Eve." Dad put a hand on her shoulder. "We'll be careful. And the edge isn't as sheer as it looks."

"That's what you always say." Her lips were a thin line as she started hiking again.

"Because it's always true." Dad tried to hold her hand, but Mom hurried past both of us to catch up to Budge and Janie.

We'll be fine, I told myself, as I picked my way more carefully over the rocky trail.

Mom wasn't talking to Dad at all by the time we reached the arch. Just to us kids, in clipped sentences.

"Sit still."

"No, you can't go with Dad."

She kept an arm around Budge and Janie both, sitting fifty feet from the cliff edge on the downward-sloping slickrock, no matter how much Janie wailed and whined. And she refused to look at the drop-off, even when Dad walked over the arch itself.

"Hurry and eat so we can hike back," she said.

On the way down Keilani and I walked together again, but quiet. Words were hard while my heart beat double-time, and I struggled to balance on noodle legs. Also with Mom so silent.

Janie, however, couldn't stop chattering about the arch.

"It was so big," she said.

"You're so big," Dad countered, not very creatively.

Janie folded her arms over her chest, bottom lip poking out. "If I'm so big, why didn't you take me on the arch?"

"Next year." Dad looked at Mom, like he was asking permission.

She didn't look at him. Didn't say anything at all.

Chapter 18

AFTER

I'm not saying anything at all—too busy panting up the switch-backs to Cohab Canyon, when Janie jumps. "Was that a rain-drop?" She squints up at the thick gray clouds.

I shake my head. "Let's get into the canyon. It's so beautiful."

She slips her hand into mine. "But we hike Cohab all the time. I want an adventure. Where are we hiking tomorrow?"

"Yeah. I'd like to see that plan of yours," Dad says. "Make sure you've got all the good stuff."

"Yeah, like Sulphur Cre—" Janie stops, looks sharply at the sky. "I felt another—"

"You didn't," I snap. "Remember? The ranger said, 'Probably not, dude.'"

"Probably does *not* mean definitely," Budge yells from the boulder he's climbing. "Like lots of times you say probably I can play *Mario* after quiet time, but then you make me do chores instead."

"Exactly." Dad laughs as he reaches up to help Budge down. "Besides, Cohab Canyon has only minimal danger of flash floods, *dudes*."

"Flash floods?" I stop in my tracks. "Minimal danger?"

"Right, *minimal*." Dad keeps walking. "It's wide, and there's plenty of room for water to go."

"Dad, if there's *any* danger, we should—"

"Trust your dad. I'll keep you safe. Promise."

Promise. There's that word again.

More of Mom's words from the day she died echo in my mind.

Keep them safe.

She said them to me, not Dad. Probably because he uses words like "minimal danger" in association with flash floods. Because he always says everything will be fine.

He also wasn't there that day—

A cool breeze blows down the trail, and I rub my arms, brushing away goose bumps along with Mom's almost-words.

Janie tugs on my arm. "We *are* hiking Sulphur Creek, right?"

"Of course," Dad says. "No trip to Capitol Reef would be complete without it."

He's right. It was Mom's favorite hike for a reason. Eight miles down the river from Chimney Rock to the visitor center—refreshing, since we hike in cool, ankle-deep water most of the way. I almost left it off, anyway, since it's pretty challenging. But Mom always said you have to pick your battles.

"Yeah," I say. "Sulphur Creek."

"And Pleasant Creek? And Grand Wash?" Janie bounces up and down.

"Yes, and yes."

"And Cassidy Arch. I looove Cassidy Arch." She digs her fingers into my arm like we're starting a roller coaster ride.

This is the battle I picked. I don't wait for Dad to chime in.

"No. We won't be doing that one."

Janie pulls her hand from mine. "What?"

"Why not?" Dad pauses to look at me.

"Too steep." I keep my tone casual as I help Budge down from his current rock.

"We can handle steep. Just proved that." Dad points to the campground, far below us.

"It's too hard to keep everyone safe without . . ."

He turns his laser eyes on me, like he heard the missing final word—Mom.

"But you promised I could walk on top of the arch this time," Janie wails.

"You can," Dad says. "We'll still do Cassidy Arch."

I can almost recite his next words along with him.

"We'll be fine," he says.

Janie high fives him. "'Cause you and me are adventurers."

It'll be nearly impossible to talk them out of it.

"I'll see if we have time on the schedule," I say.

Maybe they'll forget.

They won't.

I fold my arms across my chest. I don't need Almost-Mom rubbing it in.

Chapter 19

BEFORE

Hrishi loved to rub it in that he'd been the one to introduce us to Star Wars. Meaning he made us watch the original movies and the *Force Awakens* reboot trilogy every time he got to pick movie night because, "you can always get more out of it. There are so many layers."

He only made us watch the prequels once because even he admitted that while he liked them fine, fans in general agreed they weren't very good, and that Jar Jar Binks was an abomination. But apparently they were an important foundation for the glory that was *Clone Wars*. A glory we had yet to fully experience, to Hrishi's continual disappointment.

He'd also never really accepted me as a true fan. He'd called me *aruetii*—the Mandalorian word for outsider—ever since I refused his dare to paint the symbols of the Jedi Knights and the Rebel Alliance on the school portables in third grade. Like the excellent pencil sketch of a lightsaber I drew on his desk counted for nothing.

His fandom extended into all parts of his life, and into ours today, in the form of a giant black sign he waved from the sidelines of our soccer game while he bellowed encouragement.

It was covered with spaceships, and emblazoned with garish yellow block-font words:

SCORE ONE FOR THE REPUBLIC! GO 501ST!

Blue Thunder. I'd told him a thousand times we're not named after a legion of the Clone Army. But he'd just point out that my teammates look basically identical with their flying ponytails and matching uniforms, and that if we learned a little something about loyalty from our clone brothers, we'd win more games.

Hrishi loved soccer—watching, not playing. He couldn't dribble a ball, even if there was a free ride in an X-wing on the line. The one time he tried to run drills with me and Keilani, we schooled him hard.

I ran up the field, trying to position myself to receive Keilani's pass. She went wide, making me run like I had that gross, evil Jedi with the red face and horns on my tail.

Keilani was getting mad. Which was good and bad. It made her kicks harder, but her aim worse.

"Score one for the Republic!" Hrishi bellowed. "Scrap those Clankers!" I'm not sure how the La Roca players would feel about his comparing them to the droid army, even if they spoke nerd.

"I'm trying," I muttered. "I swear to Obi-Wan Kenobi." See? I *was* a real fan. I could say the whole name while pounding down a soccer field with my pulse rushing in my ears.

Even with the cool breeze and the thick cloud cover over-head, I was red in the face from getting *almost* to goal, then having the ball stuffed in my face.

This time, exactly like the five times before, that tall, red-headed La Roca defender appeared out of nowhere in front of me and booted the ball halfway back down the field.

Keilani growled, her rage battle cry.

I ran closer. "Shake it off."

"Why does he only cheer for you?" she muttered as I ran past.

"What?" My gaze flew to Hrishi, standing tense on the side-line like he was ready to run in the game and help.

"*Score* one for the Republic?" Her words were spiny. "Clearly cheering for you."

But there was no time to respond, not even to process her meaning.

Brianna made like her twentieth save of the game, pounding the ball halfway up the field, just as Mackelle came sprinting toward me from the sideline, yelling my name to sub out.

When I ran off the field, Mom gave me her best I'm sorry smile, and Budge and Janie raced to high five me at the pop-up shade, as I grabbed my water.

"Get rested quick." Coach kept her eyes on the game. "I need you back out there."

I nodded. Frustrating as this game was, at least Coach wanted *me* in there. Not Mackelle.

I gulped in air and water as quick as I could without doing both together.

A second later, Hrishi was beside the shade canopy, kicking my cleat gently with his worn Converse.

"You were at lightspeed out there," he said. "But I'm not sure you got the message." He danced his sign in front of me.

Score one for the Republic? Keilani had said. *Clearly cheering for you.*

I mean, I guess . . . ? Like . . . since I played forward, and she was midfield? So mostly I'd be the one to score. But what did she want the sign to say?

PASS THAT BALL TO SOMEONE ELSE WHO WILL RUN IT UP THE LINE AND THEN THEY WILL SCORE ONE FOR THE REPUBLIC?

Plus, Keilani? Jealous? About *Hrishi?* That had a big arrow on it, pointing straight at Mackelle—the current source of everything uncomfortable, unfamiliar, and just plain weird. Keilani and I both knew Hrishi would never play favorites.

Except . . . he *was* standing here with me now, waving his sign and talking about my speed while Keilani was out there actually playing.

I took a guilty step away from him. "Okay," I said. "I will attempt to score one. But for the hundredth time, we're the Blue Thunder, and we're shooting soccer balls, not phasers."

"Lasers," he corrected me. "Or possibly blasters, if you're on foot, and not in a ship."

"You're a weirdo."

"I believe you meant to ask me about where I get my delusions." His teeth were super white, grinning at me.

"Phaserbrain." I laughed at him as I deliberately messed up the insult.

"Morgan!" Coach yelled. "You ready?"

I jumped to my feet and hurried to the sideline.

"Take out Kaylee on left forward." Coach kept her eyes fixed on the field. "Get us a goal before halftime. Two minutes."

Left forward? I always played right.

"Ref! Sub!" Coach waved her hand in the air. "Go! Go!"

In a second I was back out on the field, and everything was chaos. The breeze from earlier was in a frenzy now, whipping up gusts that blew dust into our eyes, while gray mountains of clouds overhead threatened a killer rainstorm.

Our side was missing passes and running like mad and then sprinting right past the ball. I could feel the seconds spinning down to the end of the half.

When Keilani stole the ball and dribbled it up the field, I was in position. All she had to do was center it up.

"For THE REPUBLIC!" Hrishi bellowed across the field. Keilani looked right at me, her lips pressed together as she moved up the line.

I yelled at her as I backed up with feet on fire. "We got this, Kei—"

"Lani!" Mackelle yelled from right field.

Keilani paused for just a sliver of a second. She looked from me to Mackelle. Then she then sent the ball flying straight and true as always.

Straight to Mackelle.

So, instead of me, Mackelle received Keilani's pass.

Mackelle faked out that beast of a blond La Roca Defender.

And then Holy Mackelle, that fish of a girl, kicked straight as lightning, and scored one for . . . herself, probably. Like she'd even heard of the Republic.

I never scored one that day. Early in the second half, those threatening clouds got sick of talking smack and the sky broke open and dumped down in sheets until the ref declared a rainout, and we went home wet and disappointed.

I wished they'd just let us play—run in the rain until all the weird of the last hour washed right off us.

Chapter 20

AFTER

Those stupid, stupid cumulonimbus clouds that don't lie are not lying. We barely reach the mouth of Cohab Canyon up at the top of the switchbacks before fat drops of rain are pelting us.

Even Dad doesn't need convincing to turn back when he sees how much business these clouds mean.

We each take a kid by the hand, and hurry downhill as fast as we can without slipping, as the sandy trail turns to slick mud under our feet.

By the time we hit the campground, it's a full-on downpour. We sprint for the sheltered picnic tables by the Gifford Farmhouse, where two older couples huddle, laughing in surprise at the rain's violence. They step aside to allow our wild entrance.

Two minutes later we're eating ice cream under a drumming metal roof, while one of the biggest rainstorms I've ever seen— apparently only predictable by meteorologist Janie Bell—dumps down like the sky turned into a lake.

Every part of today's plan is turning to literal mud soup.

"Never fear! I've got our activity." Dad pulls out the lemon drops, and Budge and Janie's cheers echo weirdly under the corrugated tin awning.

I want to dump the whole container in the mud.

"For this lemon drop, how about you tell me your favorite thing to do with Mom. I'll start." Dad closes his eyes for a second, and takes a deep breath, his face all serious and still. Then he opens his eyes, grins brightly, and pops a lemon drop into his mouth.

"I loved camping and hiking with Mom. I know it was always my thing, more than it was hers, but . . . um . . . I think she learned to love it too." He clears his throat. "I like that it's something I introduced into her life. Morgan? You want to go?"

Lemon drops, I think. *Karaoke Consolation Parties.*

I take a step toward the pouring rain—away from Dad's hopeful smile and dangerous lemon drops.

"No. Me!" Budge squeals. "I liked when she would play *Mario* with me. Like when we would do job-level-job-level with my chores."

So many memories flood my brain. *Driving to tournament. Watching old TV shows. Reading in side-by-side hammocks.*

"Cooking dinner with her," Janie says. "It's how I decided to be a famous chef someday."

Just being near her.

Hot tears sting my eyes—blurring the farmyard even more than the driving rain.

"Morgan?" Dad prompts again.

I take another step toward the storm. "Um . . . I liked doing spontaneous things with her."

What spontaneous things? Almost-Mom's tone is so skeptical I can practically see her eyebrows challenging me.

It's true. Even the Post-Warriors-Defeat-Consolation-Karaoke Party was just the CLEANUP part of her master plan.

But that doesn't matter. I'm not doing a real lemon drop. It's just my exit strategy.

"Spontaneous things like this." I take a deep breath and sprint into the storm.

I freeze in the middle of the farmyard, gasping as thousands of heavy drops of warm, summer rain soak me to the skin in seconds, washing the tears from my cheeks like they were never there.

It takes Budge and Janie about a second to join me, laughing as they grab my hands.

"FOR THE REPUBLIC!" I yell to the liquid sky.

Then we spin and dance, turning trees and rocks and gray sky into a dizzy kaleidoscope.

We don't stop until the rain slows to a drizzle, and I slump forward, hands braced on my thighs as I catch my breath.

I put a hand over my heart, where something seems to have broken loose inside. Like an unbuttoning.

I feel free. Open.

Budge and Janie keep jumping and sliding, determined to soak up every last drop of the storm.

I meet Dad's eyes. He's smiling at me like he just found something he's been missing.

I smile back, inhaling the scent of wet grass and trees and soil. It feels like the first full breath I've taken since—I gasp.

For a moment, I totally forgot about her.

And there's the button. Closing me up, whether I want to or not.

"Let's dry off and clean up." My voice sounds stiff and strange in my ears. "That was fun, but we don't want anyone catching a chill. You could get sick."

But Budge and Janie still shriek around me, churning up red clay mud with their bare feet. Neither of them felt the button, fastening them up—closed, tight, and alone.

Budge is tearing past me when he slips. Like a slow-motion scene from a movie, I watch, helpless as he tips backward, arms pinwheeling. He plops onto his bottom in the muck, cackling with glee.

Great. This is what spontaneous gets me—a mud-fest in a national park, miles from the nearest laundromat.

Dad laughs hysterically, zero help at all.

"Stop!" I reach down to help Budge up. "You'll get mud everywhere!"

"So, they get mud everywhere." Dad walks toward me. "Don't worry about it. They're having fun. You were having fun until five seconds ago."

"Yeah!" Budge slaps his chubby five-year-old hands into the mud at his side. "Fun!"

I glare at Dad. "I could use a little backup here. There aren't any showers, or washing machines either. I only packed one pair of shorts per person per day. I wasn't planning on Mud-pocalypse."

Dad laughs. "Worst case scenario, we drive into town and do a load of laundry." He shrugs. "This is a vacation. Live a little."

"Riiight," I say. "And who's going to clean up the kids?"

"The *kids*?" He bends, scooping up a finger full of mud, and aiming at my face. "Gee. I don't know."

"Dad!" I duck away from him, but he's pretty fast for an old person.

He laughs as he grabs my arm, spinning to attack me with Mudfinger.

Budge and Janie come running.

"Get her!" Janie cheers.

"Who will clean up *the kids*? Maybe . . ." Dad tries to slime me with each word. "Their. Father. Will. Take. Care. Of. It." On the last word, he succeeds, plastering a red line down the center of my face from forehead to chin.

I stumble back, opening my mouth with difficulty, my lips glued together with thick Capitol Reef mud.

I wipe at the mud-makeup, and my fingers come away covered.

"What . . . What on earth?" I splutter.

"Having fun yet? Or do you need another dose?" Dad bends to scoop up some more.

"Another dose!" Janie jumps up and down.

Budge grabs a whole claw-full of slime, running straight for me.

"You're all nuts!" I dodge them, slipping over muddy ground until I reach the apple tree at the edge of the farmyard. Luckily Budge and Janie have short legs, and Dad's not at peak speed when he's laughing like a hyena.

I grip a low-hanging branch and launch out of their reach right as they arrive, jumping like hunting dogs treeing a fox. Only instead of baying, they chant in unison, "Get Morgan! Get Morgan!"

"Come down!" Dad's laughing so hard his face is the color of one of the sun-ripened apples hanging clustered from the branch I'm clinging to.

I shoot him a glare that hopefully looks extra fierce with my campground makeover.

"Yeah. Come down." Janie's voice is sugar-sweet, filthy hands hidden innocently behind her back.

"Get Morgan!" Budge waves his filthy hands at me. Subtlety is not his thing.

"Benjamin Michael!" I try his full name like Mom did sometimes, but he just cackles at me. Possibly the long name thing is only something Moms can use effectively.

What else would Mom do?

It's all about currency. Find what they want. Make it contingent on the desired behavior.

"Budge!" I yell. "If you don't put any mud on me, you can play video games on Mom's phone for hammock time."

"Yesss!" He jumps in the air. "Mom has *Mario* and *LEGO Star Wars* and I will not ever put any mud on you ever again."

Currency. I grin.

"Budge, no!" Janie stomps over to him. "Help me get Morgan!"

"Wait, Janie!" I yell, before she can ruin my hard work. "I'll . . . um . . . read to you."

"I can read to myself." She folds her arms.

"I'll paint your nails when we get back home. With the dot flowers."

She twists up her mouth and looks up at the sky, thinking hard.

"Seriously, Janie, what will it take for you to stop?"

Dad leans next to her ear, whispering into his cupped hand.

"Yes!" Janie folds her arms across her chest, eyes sparkling.

Why do I think she's won this battle before I've even heard her terms?

Chapter 21

BEFORE

Be careful about accepting deals without clear terms up front. I'd learned that lesson the hard way in third grade when Hrishi had used Truth or Dare to commit me to criminal activity.

I was wiser now. Hrishi? Not so much. He was teetering wildly as he walked the top rail of the fence between our yards rather than answer a question truthfully. You could almost always count on Hrishi to try the dare.

But maybe that said more about me than about him. *I* never asked *him* to do anything that could get him arrested.

This was the first time in a while that Hrishi and I had hung out alone. Since soccer season began, my life was all chores and games and practices. But after our early morning game today, Mackelle's family let her invite one friend only to the Crater hot springs in Midway, and Mackelle was sooo sorry she couldn't bring both of us. But to the shock of no one whose name starts with M and ends with -organ, she chose Keilani.

Whatever. Not like I needed more time with Mackelle. Girl was Ev-Ree-Where these days, changing the shape of Ev-Ree-Thing.

One word: trapezoid.

At least I still had Hrishi, my backyard, and Truth or Dare—three things I knew would never change.

I liked my friends like I liked my soccer team starting lineup—no surprises.

"Truth, or dare?" Hrishi leapt to the ground like the fence walk was nothing.

"Truth." I flopped back onto the trampoline, boinging gently in place. Not like there was anything I couldn't say to Hrishi.

"What's one thing you wouldn't say, even to your mom?" He sprang up onto the trampoline and sat across from me.

"Easy." I laughed. "Nothing. I tell her everything."

"Everything?" He raised an eyebrow.

"Lemon drops." I laughed. "We've got a long tradition. Plus, she's always saying this thing about better out than in. Truth, or dare?"

"Dare."

"So predictable. Four aerial somersaults in a row."

"Easy," he repeated my answer, flashing his bright, dimpled smile. He demonstrated how pitiful my challenge had been by flipping so high, I was afraid he might spin out of control and smash me to bits.

"Truth, or dare," he gasped, out of breath.

"Truth." I tried not to think about Keilani and Mackelle, snorkeling around the hot springs without me.

"You *never* take the dare!" he moaned.

"I do sometimes." Although, put on the spot like this, I couldn't remember the last time I had.

"Not anymore. You've changed." His dramatic sigh was an accusation. I felt it wiggle its irritating way under my composure.

"Have not." I folded my arms. "I'm exactly the same as I always was. Truth," I repeated.

"Who was your first crush?" He turned away from me in a bouncing circle.

First crush? I wrinkled up my nose. Had Mackelle contaminated Hrishi too?

"That one's easier than completing the Kessel Run in fifteen parsecs," I taunted him.

Both Hrishi Patel and Han Solo would have normally corrected my deliberate error from fifteen to twelve, but Han Solo remained fictional, and Hrishi just kept jump-turning in circles.

"Answer, then."

"No one. Ha!"

"No one?" He spun mid-jump and bounced to a stop.

"You knew the answer to that before you asked." I laughed. "We always make fun of *those* people."

"We do?" He looked at me like I was a math problem *before* Keilani explained it to us.

"The game doesn't work if you don't believe my answers." I folded my arms across my chest.

"It doesn't work if you answer every question with, 'No answer,'" he spat back.

"Well, you can't expect good answers if you keep asking me dumb questions." I was starting to feel too hot in the sun, and scooted to the shady side of the trampoline. Away from Hrishi.

"If my questions are so dumb, let's switch. I'll do truth, and you do dare."

I squirmed. "Let's just call Keilani, and see if she wants to—oh. Yeah. She's swimming with Mackelle." I glared at Hrishi like this was his fault, but he didn't notice, too busy trying to double bounce me to my feet.

"Scared of my dare. I repeat. You, Morgan Bell, have changed." He made it sound like I'd gone full trapezoid all on my own.

"Have not." I couldn't think straight, he was bouncing me so hard. I wobbled to my feet, where at least I could control my own movement. "Besides, you could dare me to actual vandalism again."

"That was third grade. When are you going to let that go?"

I didn't answer, too busy stealing his next bounce to launch myself higher.

"I'll go easy on you," Hrishi said. "I dare you to spin jump ten times."

I rolled my eyes, but started anyway. Quick, before he noticed *how* easy he'd gone on me and dared me to do something else.

The sky, tree branches, my house, and Hrishi swirled into dizzy scenery soup, and by the time I finished ten jump spins, I collapsed, laughing.

Hrishi showed no mercy, jumping all around me while my head spun, and I giggle-begged him to stop.

"Your turn." I laughed.

"Truth." Still jumping, he held one hand up like a courtroom swearing-in.

"About time," I said. But then I realized I hadn't thought up a question for him. Hadn't had to in a long time. "Uh . . . Who was *your* first crush?"

His feet hit the mat wrong at that moment, taking all the momentum out of his bounce. He blinked at me three times like he was a deer, and I was a set of headlights.

And then he legit stuck his tongue out at me. "No one." He bounced off the trampoline, cackling maniacally as he raced across the backyard.

"No fair," I shouted, bending to steady my still-dizzy self with my hands on my shaking knees. "I may actually barf from your stupid dare."

"You shouldn't have gone first," he hollered back, laughing as he launched himself onto our cinder-brick garden bed, then vaulted over the fence into his own backyard. "You gotta be quick with me. You're flying at sublight, while I've already made the jump to hyperspace."

Chapter 22
AFTER

Janie and Dad were a hyperspace jump ahead of me in the Mud-Attack negotiations, and I regret fighting them. What's a little mud all over your body and clothes and hair? There are rivers I could have washed in.

What I saved yesterday in slime attack, I have to pay back today by hiking Cassidy Arch.

I counteroffered with Sulphur Creek, but when we checked at the visitor center, the ranger said, "Sorry, dudes. Even without a cloud in the sky, the creek might still be too gnarly from yesterday's flash flood."

On the drive to the trailhead, I pull out my last weapon.

It's cruel—I know too well, since Janie uses this tactic on me—but I'm out of options.

"Mom said we could die on this hike."

Dad grips the steering wheel, eyes set on the scenic road in front of him. "Your mom wasn't always right," he says quietly.

I want to fight him, but it's true. Mom's broken promise to me the night she died stops the words in my mouth.

At the trailhead pavilion, a couple of other families with kids are eating lunch, and two steel-haired women with trekking poles lounge in the shade like the walk from car to picnic table was all the hike they had in them.

There's still an open table for our peanut butter and jelly lunch.

After snarfing his own sandwich in three big bites, Dad pulls out the lemon drops.

The family at the next table over has three hyper kids who have all got to be under five years old, their voices needles in my ears.

"It's a long hike," I say. "We should start."

"Today's lemon drop question?" Dad continues like I said nothing. "Tell me one thing that drove you crazy about Mom."

His question drops like a lead weight over my shoulders.

"Dad!" I shake my head at him, zipping my backpack so we can go.

"What?" He shrugs, pursing his lips in that bittersweet lemon drop smile. "It's important to remember all kinds of things about her. None of us are perfect." He pauses, and when he speaks again, his voice is quiet. "Neither was she."

"I didn't like when she made me organize my books," Janie says. "I liked them in a pile by my bed where I could reach them to read at night." Beaming, she pops a lemon drop into her mouth.

"Yeah." Budge jumps in. "And I hated how she would never let me play video games until I practiced my letters. I already know my letters. I don't need to practice them." He folds his arms, still rebellious three months later. He takes two lemon drops, darting his eyes back and forth to see if anyone caught him, but I'm too unsettled by Dad's question to bust my little brother.

Dad leans back on his hands, tipping his gaze to the sky. "You know I liked almost everything about your mom. But sometimes I did get a little tired of her ABC plans for everything. Sometimes I wanted her to just take off and do something awesome that we hadn't thought of until that second."

I stand, my face flushing with heat even here in the shade. "Her plans made us happy and safe."

I'm a hypocrite, praising ABC planning—basically my nemesis while Mom was alive. But someone's got to stand up for Mom. She's not here to defend herself, and her ABC plans were what kept us going.

They're literally the only thing I can think of to hold us together now. The only thing keeping Dad from giving up and moving us away.

Keilani's and Hrishi's faces flash into my mind.

I might have ruined everything with my two best friends, but I still don't want to leave them and move across the country. I still hope we can make up, get back to watching space operas, daring each other to do stupid things, and singing karaoke at the top of our lungs.

"You're right," Dad says. "Her plans were a great strength, and I wouldn't have changed that about her. But it doesn't mean I liked them all of the time."

"Well, I did." The lie tastes as sour on my tongue as the first lick of a lemon drop. "And I have a plan too. Today, thanks to you and Janie, it says we're hiking Cassidy Arch. So let's get started." I storm out of the pavilion to start the hike, with or without them.

Chapter 23

BEFORE

After we hiked Cassidy Arch with Keilani, Mom stayed quiet most of the day. When she turned in early with Budge and Janie, Dad suggested Keilani and I go stargazing, and we were just as glad to escape the awkward.

We lay on our backs on a blanket in the open field by the amphitheater, the black night sky spreading millions of stars from horizon to horizon.

On a night like this, you felt so small. So perfectly tiny in the middle of the universe.

"Sorry my mom was weird today," I whispered. "She gets stressy sometimes."

"Not weird," Keilani said. "Heights can be hard for people. I get it. You saw me when we found that mouse in the basement. I think the arch is like a giant, freaking, thousand-foot rodent for your mom, you know?"

"Yeah." I followed the outline of the Big Dipper all the way down to the North Star with my eyes. "But it's not usually a giant, freaking, thousand-foot rodent for me. It's like her stress was contagious today or something. I guess I'm trying to say I'm sorry *I* was weird today."

Keilani laughed softly. "You forget I've seen you eat pill bugs. I'm already familiar with your weirdness."

"One." I play-punched her bicep. "One tiny pill bug and only because stupid Kiaan Patel said girls were too wimpy to eat them."

We laughed, then went silent, and suddenly I was very small again. Lonely, even right next to Keilani.

"I meant I'm sorry I was weird because you're the one having a hard time. I'm supposed to be comforting you, and instead I was freaking out with my mom."

"Not weird. The best." She scooted closer, bonking my shoulder with hers—a sort of stargazing fist bump. "You brought me on your family vacation. So I wouldn't have to watch my mom and Tama leave me." Her voice broke on Tama's name.

I didn't know what to say then. Her hurt was my hurt, and it wrapped us up so all we could do was lie there, silent.

"You don't ever have to apologize for being weird," she said. "We're best friends forever."

"Forever." The word floated up to the sea of stars like it belonged with them.

Chapter 24

AFTER

Those first fifteen minutes on the trail to Cassidy Arch feel like forever, but it's not long before Budge and Janie pass me. They leap from rock to rock like noisy mountain goats, while I struggle to catch up—my face flaming hot as sweat drips down my forehead.

Dad's in front of me, too, but going slow like he wants to take in the view.

I hope it's not so he can bring up lemon drops again. Sharing things we didn't like about Mom was a downpour on the dry clay soil of Morgan Canyon, leaving me dangerously close to an emotional flash flood.

You should talk to him, though.

I shake my head. Mom always wanted me to talk out my feelings, but I'm not about to spill the words onto the red sand of the canyon floor for Dad to clean up—not like I did on the night of our one-and-only lemon drop.

I'm not making him feel that again. Ever.

You didn't make him. It's not your fault. She *would* say that. But I'm not sure I'd believe her, even if she were really here to say it.

"I'm so glad we're here together," Dad says over his shoulder.

"Isn't this better than clothes shopping and pencil sharpener sorting?"

Great. Now I'm thinking again about school supplies, training bras, and starting junior high.

"What? I don't get a laugh for pencil sharpener sorting?"

"Pencil sharpener sorting is no laughing matter." I try to joke, but my voice is weighed down with more than back-to-school. Like finally seeing Hrishi after all this time. Trying to find something to say. And Keilani—locked-in, best friends with Mackelle by now. Maybe I should give up and let Dad move us to Michigan.

But even thinking that makes my peanut butter and jelly lunch sit heavy in my gut.

Budge and Janie are nearly out of sight around the next switchback.

"Wait up!" I step around Dad on the path, hurrying to catch up.

"You okay?" he says.

I don't answer, because when I said, "Wait up," Budge and Janie apparently heard, "Parkour off every rock like *American Ninja Warrior—Desert Hiking Edition*."

"You guys, stop!" I yell.

I remember why I hate this hike.

Budge leaps onto a boulder too close to the edge.

Someone is going to trip and fall off a cliff.

"No!" I shout.

Budge startles, losing his balance. My muscles seize up in anticipation of his fall, but he steadies himself just in time.

"Hey!" he yells. "You messed up my wall-jump again."

My legs shake, and I steady myself on the rock to my right. He's right. I made things worse.

Why do we always have to hike somewhere our children could fall and die?

I shake my head, trying to clear the memory of Mom away.

"Get down," I pant as we reach Budge and Janie. "Wall jumping isn't safe."

"They're okay," Dad says. "It looks closer to the edge from where you're standing."

The words on the tip of my tongue are, "Tell that to Mom." But I hold them inside. What would he think if he knew how real she still is to me? How I feel her fear like it's my own?

Dad lifts Budge and then Janie to the ground. "Look. There's the arch."

My stomach drops like the sheer canyon walls beside it.

"And I get to walk on top!" Janie drags Dad forward, anxious for a closer look at her newest circus act.

Budge climbs another large rock. "Daddy, do you want to play our game?"

"What game?"

"Janie and me made it up." Budge balances precariously on one leg. "It's called Don't Fall to Your Death."

"Budge!" I gasp, horrified.

But Dad chokes back a laugh. "How do you win that one, Budge-Man?"

"You don't fall to your death," Budge says, like Dad's dumb for asking. "You want to play too, Morgan?"

"No," I snap. "And you can't either. It's not safe." I glare at Dad. Someone's got to be the responsible adult around here.

"I won't let them do anything dangerous," he says.

"Yeah!" Janie's feet grind on the rocky path as she spins to face me. "Our game is totally the opposite of not safe. Not safe is when you play *Fall* to Your Death."

All three of them crack up at this genius game idea.

"She's got you there, Morgan," Dad chortles. "Don't Fall to Your Death is clearly the preferred option. Let's play it all the time."

I take in a huge gasp of air. "It's. Not. Funny!"

Dad swivels his head toward me. "Morgan's right," he says, all humor leaving his voice. "We probably shouldn't joke about that."

I pause walking to catch my breath.

"Watch me!" Budge leaps to another rock, three feet away, leaning off the path like he's about to take flight.

"Why don't you guys climb down for a bit?" Dad's eyes stay on me, though. Not Budge, who's acting like he hasn't heard a word.

The uneven trail seems to tilt under my feet, like it's me and not Budge wobbling on the edge.

"No!" I lunge toward him. "This is not a game!" I grab him with both hands, hauling him roughly down off the rock.

"Morgaaan." Budge strains against my fists, clamped tightly onto his tee shirt.

I look up, again, see Cassidy Arch in the distance. A sudden, horrifying image fills my mind: Budge, playing this same game at the arch. Teetering on the edge of the drop-off. His small body falling down, down, down.

I clamp my teeth together against a wave of nausea.

"Let him go!" Janie pulls at my sleeve as Budge struggles to get free, but I tether him like pegs on a tent.

I squeeze my eyes tightly shut. "It's not safe!" My voice echoes back, wobbly and distorted. I've got to calm down. Got to breathe. Got to show Dad I'm okay.

"Morgan, they're safe. You're safe." It's Dad's voice, as he tries to get me to let go of Budge, who is starting to cry. But I can't seem to make my fingers relax.

Budge running, jumping. At the arch. Over the cliff.

"It's not a game. It's not."

"I know." Dad's voice is soft but firm. "You're right. It's not. Try to take a breath."

Budge. Falling, falling, falling.

"You're okay," Dad says quietly. He loosens my fingers, and Budge bounds away.

I try to walk, but I feel . . . detached. Like someone else is in my body, walking for me.

"Budge! Janie!" Dad's voice is sharp and strong. "Come back. We're taking a break."

I can't argue. I slump down right there on the path. Jagged

edges of rock jab into my back, but I don't care. I put my hand to my head, where I feel hot and cold at the same time. My fingers come away wet with sweat. A trickle runs down my back.

"Breathe, sweetheart. In through your nose. Out through your mouth." Dad's hand is on my shoulder, the other smoothing hair away from my face.

The canyon swirls around me, red rocks and blue sky mixing like spilled paint. I open my mouth as wide as I can, but nothing will give me enough air.

Then suddenly Budge and Janie squish in on either side, making a Morgan sandwich. I flinch away, claustrophobic.

"Give her some space," Dad says.

Then one of them starts singing. I'm not sure whether it's Budge or Janie, but it doesn't matter. Because pretty soon it's both of them, and then Dad too. And what they're singing is "Edelweiss."

Mom's song for me.

Their voices fill my lungs like oxygen, and I've never been so grateful for a breath.

After a few moments, another almost-voice joins them—Mom.

They sing the song three times straight through.

When I finally look up, Dad squats in front of me, hand still on my shoulder. "You okay, sweetheart?"

I nod, not trusting my voice.

"Okay," he says—not like he believes me. That line between

his eyebrows is so deep, eyebrows squinched close together. "I think this is enough of a hike for today. Let's turn back."

My jaw drops.

You always finish the hike. One foot in front of the other.

"But Dad!" Janie says. "I get to walk on top. You promised."

"I know." His eyes flicker back down to me. "But it'll be better next year, when you're a little older."

"But Morgan's fine. See?"

"Yeah." I try to stand on newborn deer legs. "I'm fine."

This was the one thing Janie wanted, and I'm ruining it.

"We'll try again another time," Dad says.

"Nooo." The sound of Janie's voice echoes off the canyon walls, and all the way to the middle of my chest. Brokenhearted, like her crying last night.

This time it's my fault, and that knowledge hurts worse than the cramps in my lungs when I was trying to breathe and panicking instead.

"We can finish the hike." I try to stop the trembling aftershocks of the panic attack.

But Dad shakes his head, smiling sadly. "Not today."

Chapter 25

BEFORE

"**N**ot today." Mom pursed her lips. "I'm sorry, but I need you to watch Budge and Janie."

"But this is the first Saturday in forever with no soccer. Last week Keilani was away with Mackelle. And we can finally hang out—just the two of us."

"Look, Morgan, I've got to record a video for my channel. Your dad's at the office working toward the new software launch, and I'm past deadline for a guest blog post. Plus, my head is splitting. Can't the two of you have fun hanging out *with* your brother and sister?"

I sighed. It wasn't a straight-up order, but it might as well have been.

So, while Budge and Janie made themselves sick on the merry-go-round, Keilani and I sat and "talked" on creaking swings that had more to say than we did.

Things had been weird since the rain game. I'd thought hanging out, just the two of us, would fix things. But here I sat with questions in my mouth, and no way to speak them into the silence.

Why is Mackelle always hanging out with us?

Why are you being so weird about Hrishi?

What was Mr. Morton's deal showing all those Octonauts clips in science last week?

Well . . . that one I could have said, but every time I opened my mouth to speak, I'd picture the moment just before that pass—Keilani looking from Mackelle to me, seeing me wide open, and sending the ball straight up the field to Mackelle.

After a bit, Keilani started swinging for real, pumping her long legs back and forth. I followed, and before long, it was a contest.

"Ha!" I shrieked. "I'm higher than you."

"Not a chance!"

I laughed. This felt good. Safe, familiar.

"What are you guys doing?" a nasally voice said behind us.

A judgy, nasally voice that sounded disgusted to find two twelve-year-old girls swinging like babies at the park.

Mackelle? I turned to question Keilani with my eyebrows.

She shrugged and dragged her foot to stop her swing.

I stopped pumping, quickly losing steam.

"You two are like little kids." Mackelle pursed her fishy lips. "It's adorable."

Keilani looked down at her feet, embarrassed.

Was this the same girl who'd belted "Let It Go" at the amphitheater last summer, blowing kisses at random boys?

"Anyways," Mackelle said. "Thanks for texting me to come over."

I shot an accusing look at Keilani, who didn't meet my eyes.

I guess I didn't explicitly tell her not to invite Mackelle, but I shouldn't have to.

"I was sooo bored," Mackelle whined. "I was even thinking of dyeing my hair. Do you think pink would look good on me?"

Keilani nodded. "Probably. Tama dyed her hair with that streak of purple, and it looks good."

"I don't know." I pretended to consider it. Was pink really the best hair color for a know-it-all friendship invader?

"Yeah," Mackelle said. "Tama's pic was my inspiration."

Huh. Keilani didn't show *me* the picture of Tama's new hair.

"I should get home soon," I said. "Hrishi's making me finish season four of *Clone Wars* tonight."

"*Hri-shi*," Mackelle sang his name.

"What?"

"See, Keilani." Mackelle raised her eyebrows. "Told you she likes him."

"Of course I like him," I said. "He's one of our best friends. Mine and Keilani's." I couldn't resist reminding her of our triangle—a shape with *three* points—formed long before she showed up. And built to last long after she moved on.

"*Morgan and Hrishi, sitting in a tree*," Mackelle chanted.

"Eew. Don't be gross."

"Leave her alone," Keilani warned, shaking her head at Mackelle.

"Gross?" Mackelle actually cackled then. "Oh, poor Hrishi! He was right, wasn't he? She seriously doesn't see it." Using her fist as a microphone, she belted out the opening riff of "You Don't

Know You're Beautiful," the song Hrishi and I sang together after the Warriors game.

My face was on fire. "Because we sang together? You're getting all weird because we sang a song?"

My eye-lasers blasted one question at Keilani. *This is the person you want us to hang out with*?

"Morgan's right," Keilani said quickly. "Hrishi is our friend. End of story." But her words weren't as convincing, spoken as they were to her flip-flops.

"Aww." Mackelle smirked. "You two are so cute. And *so* in denial. Junior high is going to blow your minds. You think you can stay friends with a boy? That's not how it works. And you think a cute guy like Hrishi will stay unattached? Not in *junior high*."

Even though my swing was still, I felt motion sick. She didn't have to keep saying *junior high* like she'd say *Jupiter*.

"Hrishi isn't unattached," I muttered. "He's attached to me and Keilani."

Triangle.

"Except Keilani and I both know he wants to be more attached to one of you than the other." She rubbed her high-gloss lips together.

Keilani gave Mackelle her very shut-up-est of looks. It was unmistakable. At least to her *real* BFF.

But Mackelle was not in a shutting-up mood.

"Me and Lani heard him telling his big brother at karaoke night—"

"Morgan!" Budge shouted from the slide. "Janie's making me play My Little Pony."

"Am not! He wanted to."

"Yes she is, and I'm bored. Can we go home now?"

"One minute," I hollered back, not taking my eyes from Mackelle and Keilani. If we didn't leave soon, Mackelle would be picking wood chips out of her lip gloss, but I needed to know what they'd heard first. "What did Hrishi say?"

Mackelle glared at Budge for interrupting her drama. "Annnywaaays, Hrishi told Kiaan it doesn't matter if he likes you. That you'd never notice him. That you only think of him as a friend." Her lips turned down in a shiny pout. "Poor guy. You should have seen his face."

My mouth fell open.

Hrishi?

She had to be lying.

But when I looked at Keilani, she was still staring at the ground, silently grinding wood chips to sawdust with her feet.

"Truth, or Dare?"

"Truth."

"Who was your first crush?"

"No one."

"No one?"

The whole playground seemed to move around me, as I lurched unsteadily to my feet.

"Morgaaan," Budge and Janie yelled in tandem.

"One. Minute!" I looked at Keilani again.

She mouthed one silent word—"*Sorry*."

This time I was the one who looked away.

"I hate to say it," Mackelle said in her giddy-to-say-it voice. "But boys have short attention spans. I'd do something quick to show Hrishi you've noticed." She gave me a pitying look. "Or he'll move on to someone who has."

I didn't even respond. Just left to take Budge and Janie home. Where I would find an old soccer ball, pump it up, and then kick it against my house until it exploded.

Chapter 26

AFTER

A couple of hours of booting my soccer ball over the wide, grassy field in the middle of the campground is what I really need right now. But I deliberately left my ball off the packing list—not wanting the daily reminder that I don't play anymore.

Plan B is in ruins. I don't know how to CLEANUP to get us out of Plan C, and it feels like we're headed for Plan D—DISASTER.

Dad's acted a little Foggy since we bailed on the hike, but I still hammock-nap all afternoon to avoid him, while he plays card games with Budge and Janie and buys us ice cream as a consolation for missing the arch.

Over our canned vegetable soup dinner, he watches me with worried, full-focus eyes. And before bed, he tells me to wait by the fire while he tucks in Budge and Janie so we can talk.

I feel like I did in May, waiting in the principal's office with Mr. Yamamoto for Mom to come pick me up after Morgan's Stupidest Decision Ever.

Dad takes the chair across from me and snaps on the red lantern. The fluorescent bulb flares erratically to life, and I blink against the glare.

He holds out the open canister of lemon drops and raises an eyebrow.

I twist my principal's office hands together in my lap and shake my head.

Janie's giggles and Budge's answering squeals reach us from the tent, along with the rubber-squeaking sounds of them bouncing on our air mattresses.

Dad laugh-sighs, shaking his head. The dim light from the lantern makes his face all spooky-ghost-story-tellerish. He pops a lemon drop into his own mouth, sucking on the candy in silence.

It's like he's waiting for it to turn sweet before he can talk.

"It turns out I'm not a perfect parent." He makes the sign of an explosion by his temple, like this information will blow my mind.

I attempt a laugh.

"I know. Hard to believe." He's always more comfortable with the silly stuff. "It's just . . . I'm kind of feeling around in the dark, trying to figure all of this out alone. Without your mom, you know? Budge and Janie are still pretty easy. I can cheer them up by spelling weird words or buying ice cream."

I nod.

"But you have more stuff going on. More stuff hurting you. And it's not like you have to tell me everything, but—" He waits like he hopes I'll do just that.

When I don't, he sighs. I hate how sad he looks.

"I'm worried about you, Morgan, and I feel like I've really messed up. This summer kind of just . . . slipped away from me.

I kept trying to find help to take the burden off you, because I know you're carrying way more than someone your age should—"

I knew my panic attack today would make him worry. Make him start trying to fix everything.

"I'm fine." I force a bright smile that probably looks creepy in the lantern light. "Really. I just wasn't feeling well today. You don't need to worry."

"You say you're fine. But . . . did you know that until today, I haven't heard you talk about your mom in over a month?"

"I talk about her." I fold my arms across my chest.

Dad shakes his head.

"What? Like you're keeping track?" I'm mostly joking but—

"Yeah." He looks right into my eyes. "Alejandro asked me to keep notes of certain things on a calendar when I met with him in July."

The darkness hiding the canyon walls thickens, pressing in on me.

"You met with Alejandro . . . in July?"

"Yeah. A couple of times."

My skin prickles. "But I haven't needed to visit him since June."

I remember that first meeting after my panic attack—me and Dad in Alejandro's warm, cozy office while they mostly talked, and I mostly tried not to cry.

We're a team, Alejandro had said. *Me, and you, and your dad. Working together to help you be happy and safe.*

I just hadn't imagined the team would meet without its star player.

"I went to see Alejandro because I'm worried. Because I want you to be happy."

I know he's trying to comfort me, but I've just spent three months trying to show Dad I'm happy. Help *him* be happy, when all the time he could see right through me. I grip the canvas arms of the chair so tight my knuckles hurt.

"I went to see Alejandro because whenever I try to talk to you, whenever I ask how you're doing, you say you're fine."

A gust of wind rustles the leaves of the cottonwood overhead, washes goose bumps over me. I wrap my arms around myself to defend against the chill, and this feeling that's colder than evening desert breeze on my bare arms.

"I *am* fine."

"Exactly," Dad says, like I proved his point.

Then we glare at each other for a second. Well . . . *he* mostly looks worried. I'm definitely glaring.

"I don't think you're fine," he says as gently as you can say something like that. "And Alejandro doesn't think you're fine either."

My lips tremble and my teeth start trying to chatter.

If I'm not fine, what does that make me?

"I needed your mom," Dad says. "Budge and Janie needed her. We all miss her. But you . . . losing your mom at this point in your life. I'm worried that . . ."

His voice trails off like it would be too awful to say what he's afraid of.

He puts a hand on my shoulder, but I pull away fast. I can't be touched right now. I'm made of hard, cold glass and I'll break if anyone comes near me.

Dad and Alejandro think I can't survive without Mom. They think I'll break. Or I'm already broken.

Broken.

The word jangles around in my brain. Sharp and jagged.

I'm so broken Dad needs a "team" to help him help me.

So broken I can't let my dad touch me. So broken I can't finish a hike without a panic attack.

So broken I'll never survive life without Mom.

Darkness presses in at the corners of my vision. I'm seeing Dad down a tunnel.

What made me think I could fix things for anyone else?

"But Alejandro has good ideas for how to help you," Dad says brightly.

"Like . . . writing what I talk about on a calendar." The words sound like they're coming from outside me.

He nods.

"Like bringing the lemon drops and asking specific questions."

He nods again.

"Like taking me camping where we always went with Mom?" My voice breaks on those words. I can't be the reason we're here.

He watches me for a second, and I go very still.

I already know the answer.

All this time I was trying to fix everything for everyone, when the whole point of this trip was to fix *me*.

I'm not the solution. I'm the problem.

My whole vision is dark, except for the spot of light where Dad sits, clasping and unclasping his hands and endlessly watching me.

"Maybe it was a bad idea to come here so soon," Dad says. "Maybe we should go home."

A rising tide of emotion strains against the dam I've built— ready to come pouring out.

Talking about it might be a good thing. Almost-Mom's voice is gentle as the breeze, ruffling my hair against my face.

No.

If Dad and Alejandro already think I'm not fine, what will they think, what will they decide they have to *do* when they see the swirled-up emotion soup inside me?

But—

No.

If Dad finds out how fine I'm really not, everything— *everything* that's still familiar in my life will change, and no amount of planning will stop that.

I swallow back the flood of sadness, disappointment in myself, fear that Dad's giving up on me. I take a deep breath. In through the nose, out through the mouth—the one Alejandro idea still working for me.

Calm.

So calm.

Not freaking out.

I lift my gaze, make eye contact. "I'm fine," I say again. He won't believe it, so I try to soften it. "Not totally fine." I look away because the understatement is one of the biggest lies I've ever told. "But . . . uh . . . fine, you know? Okay. And the camping trip is fine too. We should totally stay."

We have to stay. I need a few more days to prove I can do this.

Dad waits so long I'm about to lose control of my fine, fine, fine expression.

"Please," I whisper.

The please does him in. His lips quirk up in a sad attempt at a smile.

"Fine, huh?" He raises an eyebrow like he doesn't believe me, but like he knows that's all I'm going to say.

I nod.

He sighs, leaning forward to put his arms around me. I let him this time.

I don't say anything. I can't. Not now that I know he thinks I'll never make it without Mom.

That fear was easier to carry when it only belonged to me.

Chapter 27

BEFORE

I never passed up the chance for a lemon drop when I needed one. I'd learned long before that Mom was right. No matter how sour the subject, if I talked it out, the sweet came—usually right away.

But all the way home from the park, I barely heard Janie's relentless chatter over Mackelle's words, on loop in my mind. Words I couldn't even fully understand myself, much less explain to Mom.

Junior high is going to change everything.

You think you can just stay friends with a boy?

I'd do something quick to show Hrishi you've noticed. Or he'll move on to someone who has.

I held a hand over my stomach where her words churned like rotten food.

I wasn't even sure what having a crush felt like, but I was pretty sure that wasn't what I felt with Hrishi.

Just the thought that Mackelle might be right made me feel like I was about to barf.

I'd just forget it, except for two things.

1. Keilani didn't tell Mackelle she was wrong. She didn't say anything.

2. Truth or Dare: *Who was your first crush?*

When I'd asked about Hrishi's crush, he was gone faster than Keilani can boot a soccer ball halfway up the field.

When we got home and Budge and Janie scampered off for screen time, I flopped down on the couch, hugged a throw pillow to my face, and let out a low growl.

A minute later, someone snatched the pillow away.

It was Mom, holding out a lemon drop.

I shook my head.

Usually lemon drops waited until we asked for them. Today her raised eyebrows weren't so patient.

I took the lemon drop, but didn't put it in my mouth.

Maybe because—as I'm sure Mackelle would have happily reminded me—only babies who weren't ready for junior high needed to suck on candy while they talked about feelings with their mommy.

"It's nothing," I said.

"Didn't sound like nothing. Sounded like you were turning into a dinosaur or something."

She was trying to make me laugh.

But . . . *Hrishi and Morgan, sitting in a tree?* I clamped my claw-fingers tight around the pillow like I was wringing its neck.

Maybe I *was* turning into a dinosaur.

I sighed. "It's just Mackelle."

"Ah." Mom nodded.

This wasn't the first Mackelle-inspired lemon drop.

Mom sat there, waiting for me to open up and tell her everything, like I always did.

"The thing is . . ."

Mackelle's slippery, twisty words and Keilani's shoe-gazing and next-to-nothing-saying formed a lump in my throat.

I shrugged.

Mom put an arm around my hunched-up shoulders. "This is a hard time of life." It was like she understood everything, without my saying a word. "And friends can be the hardest part of all."

"Mackelle's not my friend," I muttered. Those words felt true, no matter how quietly I said them.

"That's important information to have," Mom said. "It can be hard to tell, sometimes, who your true friends are."

"Yeah."

Keilani, texting Mackelle to come so she wouldn't be alone with me, showing Tama's new hair to Mackelle and not to me.

Keilani, hearing Hrishi say he liked me, and not telling me so I had to find out from Mackelle.

Keilani, sitting silent in her swing, pulverizing wood chips with her sneakers.

A goose bump–cold thought shivered over my skin.

What if Keilani didn't want to be best friends with me anymore?

What if she already wasn't?

What if she'd already chosen Mackelle?

And what if Hrishi had stupidly decided junior high meant he had to either *like* like me, or quit liking me altogether?

What if instead of my perfectly balanced triangle, or even an ugly trapezoid, I was just a dot? Just me, alone?

"Just know I'm team Morgan for life," Mom said like she always did. "You can talk about whatever it is when you're ready."

I should. Suck on a lemon drop until the sour turned sweet and Mom could help me untangle the twist of Mackelle's words.

I opened my mouth to do it, but I just . . . couldn't.

Not yet.

Mom could help me later, after I'd had a little more time to work it out for myself.

Chapter 28

AFTER

Sleeping on cold, hard ground, listening to raindrops drum on your tent turns minutes into years. Especially with one excruciating sentence cycling through your mind: *I don't think you're fine, and Alejandro doesn't think you're fine either.*

If I'm not fine, the last thing Mom asked of me is something I can never do.

So I'm fine. I have to be.

When the sun finally lights the sky, I offer to brush Janie's hair into the high ponytail she's always asking for. When Budge needs help spelling *Koopa*, *Big Bowser*, and *booger*, I do it without saying, "What the heck?" And I swallow my gluey oatmeal without a word of complaint.

Dad doesn't want me to say I'm fine, so I'll show him instead.

Today's sky is blue, cloud-free. So, I optimistically put on my water sandals and tell Dad we're hiking Sulphur Creek.

What better way to show I'm capable of carrying out my plan than successfully finishing everyone's favorite, most adventurous hike?

Dad doesn't meet my eyes. "First I need to chat with the ranger about hike options."

Hike options? We've got maps of the whole park printed in our brains.

I take in a breath to protest, but arguing wouldn't make me seem fine. So, I let out the air, slow and steady through my smiling teeth.

I bring everyone's water sandals anyway.

At the visitor center, Janie hops out of the van, wearing her fully loaded Hiking Survival Backpack. I can't imagine why she thinks she'll need it. Is she anticipating a granola bar emergency while Dad grabs a trail map?

"Dudes!" The big ranger with the long curly hair leans across a glass countertop covered in brochures. "Bet you guys loved Cassidy Arch."

Budge blurts, "We didn't see the arch because Morgan freaked out."

"Bummer, dude. You'll have to try aga—"

Budge interrupts. "It rained on us and we played in the mud and then me and Janie walked all the way back to our tent naked." He grins like he's describing the best day of his life. Of course he doesn't mention that the nude trek was ten feet from the picnic table where we stripped them.

"Whoa. TMI, Dude." The ranger straightens up.

"What's TMI?"

"Tooo much information. Definitely did not need to know that."

"Actually," Dad says, "we're here for more ideas of what to do around the park."

"*Actually*," I jump in, "we want to know if we can do Sulphur Cre—"

"Can we become Junior Rangers?" Janie speaks over me.

"Whoa." The ranger pushes back a brown curl that's slipped out of his ponytail. "One camper at a time."

"Junior Rangers!" Janie insists.

I shake my head, pointing at the three Junior Ranger patches already sewn to her backpack.

"Great idea, Janie," Dad says quickly. "Can we get three packets?"

He did *not* just get me a Junior Ranger packet.

"Two," I correct him.

Budge and Janie race to the table, eager to start their self-inflicted homework.

Dad doesn't seem to notice my ranger-rage.

Which is good, I remind myself, smoothing my expression.

"What about Sulphur Creek?" I ask—calmly, like I don't really care.

"Oooh, Sulphur Creek?" Ranger Dude rubs his stubble. "Flash flood danger is lower today, but—"

"No. We're going to wait on that one." Dad tries to smile at me. "Morgan, could you help Janie and Budge with their packets?"

His words are a bucket of cold water, dumped over my head.

Go sit at the baby table, Morgan. Let the adults plan things.

I slouch over to the tables, slumping into a chair so short my knees fold up against my chest.

"Wanna help with my geology bingo?" Budge asks.

I shake my head, focused on Dad and the ranger.

"We need something gentler," Dad says. "Cassidy Arch was a bit more than our crew could handle."

I stiffen in my baby chair.

"Dude." The ranger nods super slow. "I totally get it. What with the public nudity and all, I'd say so."

Dad laughs. "What do you have that's still fun, but . . ." He lowers his voice. "Wouldn't make anyone anxious?"

I squirm in my kiddie chair as Ranger Dude tosses out bland ideas like Ripple Rock Nature Center, the pioneer schoolhouse, and petroglyphs. They're setting up a baby version of our favorite family vacation.

"Also, if you haven't seen our visitor center movie about the effects of water on the land, you have not lived. Amazing footage of Capitol Reef. Out of the heat and in the air-conditioning, dude."

Dad always says if you're in nature, you should be in nature. Not watching pictures of nature. He'll say no.

But then I hear his response. "Sounds good."

I freeze.

I feel like I just got mercy rolled. Like when we ended the Rocky Mountain game early to put them out of their misery.

I won't get another chance to prove to Dad I can handle this.

Chapter 29
BEFORE

You shouldn't have to prove anything to someone who's known you forever.

My plan for dealing with Mackelle's nonsense about Hrishi was to keep being the person he was friends with in the first place.

"Hey, girl." Mackelle greeted me on the playground at lunch. "Wanna sit on the monkey bars?"

I sighed. I'd hoped Mackelle would glom on to someone else since Keilani was at her math club meeting.

"I was going to play." I gestured over at the 9 Square frame, where Hrishi was already lined up, waving me over. I held up one finger in response—getting rid of Mackelle would just take a second.

"With *the boys*?" she giggled.

I shrugged, not about to let her get in my head. "You can come if you want." It was an empty invitation. We both knew how Mackelle felt about sweating at school.

"Morgan," Hrishi yelled. "Come on. Line's getting long!"

Mackelle waved back at him, giggling loudly.

"Do you have to make everything weird?"

She put a hand on her hip. "You can't blame *me* for things changing. Boy and girl stuff. It changes. Keilani agrees with me. She says Tama told her all this stuff before I did."

My shoulders rose toward my ears—stiffening me into a tight-wound Morgan statue.

"Look, even *if* you're right and Hrishi has a crush on me, no way it's something weird and romantic like you've been saying," I hissed. "It's *Hrishi.*"

"And *Hrishi* is a *boy.* While *you* are a *girl.*" Mackelle announced like the shock might shatter my world. "Boys and girls pair up. It's what they do."

I shuddered, picturing next-door Hrishi, glued to some other girl by interlocked fingers. Everyday, comfortable Hrishi, replaced by someone who makes goo goo eyes and leaves flowers in lockers.

It wasn't like I wanted him leaving flowers for me, and I'd probably die laughing if he gave me some movie-style romantic look. I just wanted my triangle. Was that too much to ask?

"Even if he doesn't find another girlfriend in the first five minutes of junior high—and I mean, look at the guy." Mackelle gestured toward Hrishi, who had given up on waiting for me and was almost in the top spot on 9 Square already. "Everything will get awkward between you anyway. Keilani says it already is."

I growled. Out loud.

"If anything is weird between us, it's that he thinks I've changed," I said. "Like I'm not as fun anymore, not taking risks or dares. That I'm spending too much time with—" My mouth fell open. "That's it!"

"What's it?" She wrinkled her nose up at me.

I just stared at her.

I couldn't exactly tell her that if Hrishi was feeling anything at all right now it wasn't that he wanted me to be his sixth-grade *girlfriend*—whatever that even meant. That the problem was too much Mackelle in our triangle. He had to be feeling like the forgotten fourth point of a trapezoid.

Just. Like. Me.

"You *do* like him." She smiled, slow and coy, like a smug, friend-stealing right forward who wanted to eat rubber playground mulch. "And I'm serious. You'd better show him, or he'll—"

"Whatever." I waved her sly words aside, as my brain replaced the image of lovesick Hrishi with the real image—the Hrishi who was as worried about our friendship as I was.

"Okay," I said. "Let's say I *did* want to show him I like him."

Mackelle clapped her purple sparkle-nailed hands together. "Do something big. A grand gesture!" She squealed. "It may be a little over the top, but that's what it takes to get someone's attention. Oooh, you *do* like him. I was riii-iiight."

"Shh. Calm down." I darted a glance toward 9 Square to make sure Hrishi was safely occupied. "I don't *like* like him. I just want to show him I'm still the same Morgan he's always known. That I'm still his friend, you know?"

I could tell by the giddy foot-patter of her happy dance that she did *not* know. But we could agree to disagree.

She could think whatever she wanted, and I could still be right. I didn't need her approval of my plan.

And I did have a plan. A tiny spark of a perfect plan—just starting to form.

Keilani was going to think I'd gone nuts.

But my plan would show Hrishi I hadn't changed—if I was brave enough to do it.

Truth, or dare? Hrishi in my mind laughed. Shorter then, but same dimples.

Dare. A younger me braced for impact.

I wasn't ready for his dare back in third grade. But now?

"Mackelle," I said. "Do you have any spray paint? I might need to do some art."

Chapter 30

AFTER

The Capitol Reef water movie is hardly the work of art the ranger described, but Janie and Budge like all screens, so we sit and watch. It doesn't take long, however, for all those images of flash floods, and water pockets, and the drip, drip, drip of erosion to overpower Janie's bladder.

Dad doesn't want her using the outdoor bathrooms alone, so I stand in the warm sun just outside, holding her backpack and stewing.

Today would be perfect for hiking Sulphur Creek—not a cloud in the sky.

When Janie comes out, I'm not ready to head back into the cold, dark theater. She forgets her backpack in her hurry to catch the movie's end.

In front of the visitor center, one of the best views in Capitol Reef spreads out like a giant mural, with Castle Rock looming large as a real fortress.

Will you look at that, Morgan? It never gets old.

It feels like Almost-Mom is really with me, taking in the view we always see at the end of the Sulphur Creek hike.

The trail begins a mile up the road at Chimney Rock, quickly meeting up with the creek, then winding through eight miles of canyon and over the three waterfalls. It ends right behind this visitor center. And it's not on the park brochure, so usually we're alone the whole way.

The world's only perfect hike.

We can't have a successful camping trip to Capitol Reef without Sulphur Creek. And even after yesterday, I know I can still do it.

If I can show Dad I'm brave enough to do this hike, maybe he'll believe in me again.

A tiny spark of a thought—dangerous and electric—ignites in my mind.

I check the time on my phone.

Ten thirty. Still plenty of daylight left to finish the hike.

Goose bumps tingle over my arms.

I could slip away right now, walk to the trailhead, and show them all I can still do challenging things without dissolving into a pool of anxiety.

Suddenly, Mackelle's voice is in my head: *it may be a little over the top, but that's what it takes to get someone's attention.*

Following Mackelle's advice feels like letting the opposing team call your plays, but I guess she might not be wrong about everything.

I look down at Janie's ever-prepared backpack slung over my arm, and at my toes, sticking out of my water sandals. It's like the universe itself is offering the chance to prove myself.

I'm going to take it.

You shouldn't have to prove yourself to someone who's known you forever. Almost-Mom echoes my own thoughts. Probably because so many of them started with her that it's hard to tell the difference.

I wave my hand, brushing her nagging voice aside.

I'm going to sneak inside and leave a note with Budge, so Dad won't worry I was kidnapped or something. Then I'll top off Janie's hydration pack, and walk the mile to Chimney Rock.

Then I, Morgan Elizabeth Bell, will hike Sulphur Creek alone.

Chapter 31

I should have been brave enough to do this alone. But Mackelle insisted on coming, and once Keilani realized I was serious, and she offered her reluctant company, I wasn't strong enough to refuse.

Neither of them were helping settle my nerves.

"You don't have to do this," Keilani said for like the eleventh time. "It was a ridiculous idea in third grade. It's even worse now, when we should definitely know better."

"Sometimes ridiculous is what we need to get someone's attention." Mackelle stretched up on tiptoes, sticking the final piece of blue painter's tape on the outline of the third and final Star Wars symbol—Rex's clone helmet with those weird eyes, the Mandalorian symbol for "warrior." The rebel and Jedi symbols anyone would recognize, but this third one . . . I was counting on only Hrishi to understand.

"I still don't even *want* Hrishi's attention," I moaned. "Other than just getting back to normal so we can act like regular humans, and he'll know I'm still me—still all-in."

"*All-in.*" Mackelle staggered swoonily off the step stool.

"All-in for *friendship*," I snapped. "Get a grip, Mackelle."

She shot Keilani a looook.

Agree to disagree, I reminded myself.

I checked out the four-foot-tall symbols, now outlined in blue tape on the outside wall of the sixth-grade portable.

Mackelle had provided the tape, leftover from last year, when they'd transformed her pink-and-purple baby room into something that didn't make her want to barf her world-wise sixth-grade guts out.

Now I felt like barfing my own totally-not-ready-for-seventh-grade guts out.

I clutched the can of burgundy spray paint too tight with my shaking hand.

"Wait, gloves!" Mackelle whipped out a pair. "So you won't get incriminating paint marks on your hands."

"I thought you said true art isn't vandalism." I accepted the gloves anyway.

When I'd freaked out and almost backed out of the plan entirely, Mackelle had assured me that her *middle school* art teacher Mrs. Setzer said if you're a true street artist like that guy Bunksy or Bankers or whatever, your art is a welcome addition to the world.

"Right." She nodded too quickly. "But even Banksy stays anonymous."

Keilani darted her eyes around the abandoned, dusk-lit schoolyard. "We can still rip down the tape and go home."

I dare you. Third-grade Hrishi with his bright smile.

You've changed. Sixth-grade Hrishi, looking at me like I just said all the clones were basically the same.

"For the Republic," I breathed, staring at the four-foot-high tape grid.

I was going to do it—take the dare. Do this terrifying, hopefully-not-illegal, totally un-Morgan-like thing. For what?

So Hrishi would know we were still friends. That I was still the same Morgan as always?

So he'd realize I noticed him?

Which, until Mackelle suggested otherwise, I thought he knew just fine.

"You want me to help you paint?" Keilani probably meant the offer, but her voice was an underinflated soccer ball.

That was the moment I almost ripped down the tape and ran away. As dumb as she thought this was, she was willing to help me anyway? Maybe some things never changed.

"We can't, silly." Mackelle pulled her toward their lookout spot in the bushes. "This is Morgan's grand gesture. Between her and her man."

"*Mackelle! Eew.*" What was wrong with her?

She just laughed.

Keilani watched me, her expression unreadable. But I knew she'd still help if I asked.

I gave her a weak smile and a shaky thumbs-up—all I could manage with my body's fight-or-flight response to this wild situation.

Truth? Flight was looking pretty good, at the moment.

Dare?

Sixth-grade Hrishi's face popped into my mind again—dimples on parade, head cocked to the side, his whole face a question.

This was the nuttiest thing I'd ever done. But if it helped me keep Hrishi safe in my triangle, it would be worth it.

"It's okay." I smiled bravely at her. "I should probably do this on my own."

Chapter 32

AFTER

This hike is the nuttiest thing I've ever done on my own. Every step along the road to Chimney Rock on the shoulder of Capitol Reef's winding highway feels surreal, dangerous. Floods of adrenaline tell my shaky-legged body to turn around and run back to Dad. And every time a car pulls past, I'm sure it *is* Dad, that he's read the note, guessed where I've gone, and come to stop me.

I can't get caught now.

Unfinished, this hike does not prove I'm fine.

It's a one-way ticket back to weekly meetings with Alejandro, Dad's face perma-lined with worry, and—no. I won't think about us moving to Michigan.

I've got this.

My note to Dad was carefully nonspecific:

Dear Dad,
~~Do not worry.~~
Needed a walk by myself to clear my head.
I'll be back to camp in a few hours.
I'm totally safe. Promise.

- Morgan

I had to cross off the bit about not worrying, because the proven best way to make a parent worry is to tell them not to.

The note isn't actually a lie. I do need to clear my head, I will be walking, and I said a few hours, which I'm pretty sure means up to five. I should have plenty of time.

Only one word in the note makes me cringe.

Promise.

There are things you shouldn't promise because you can't a hundred percent control them.

But Dad hiked alone for weeks on the Great Western Trail, and he said it showed him what he was capable of.

It probably showed other people in his life too.

Before anyone can stop me, I make it to Chimney Rock. None of the tourists milling around the parking lot notice me at all, and Dad doesn't screech up in our family van to ask what on earth I was thinking.

So, I slip across the road and descend into the dried-out stream bed that leads to Sulphur Creek—out of sight and on my way.

Chapter 33

BEFORE

"What on earth were you thinking?" Mom's hands gripped the steering wheel so hard her knuckles turned white.

I slumped in the passenger seat, trying hard not to cry.

The vice principal, Mr. Yamamoto, had spotted me on the school security cameras, and shut down my artistic debut before I could free-hand the eyes onto Rex's helmet. Then he'd called Mom, and now here we were.

"Mackelle said—"

"Nope." Her voice was sharp. "You own your own choices. Did Mackelle vandalize the school, or was that you?"

I slumped in my seat, miserable. "Me."

"Right. *You* made a choice." She stopped at a red light, turning to look right at me. Dark circles shadowed her eyes. "So you must have thought this through, right? Because the Morgan I know doesn't do things like this, ever. So, explain to me—clearly, so I can understand—what you were thinking."

"I wasn't." I folded my arms, protecting the lie.

I *was* thinking—too hard about too many things.

"But you painted giant Star Wars symbols on the side of the portable?" Her words were a challenge.

I clamped my teeth shut, nodding.

"Was Hrishi involved?"

I sucked in a quick breath, looking over at her. Did she know?

But I couldn't read her expression.

I shook my head. Another lie.

He was involved, just not in the way she thought.

He didn't know anything about it—yet.

My face flamed, hot.

One look at the mess I'd made, and the whole thing seemed ridiculous.

They didn't even look like the original symbols when I was finished—just amorphous, drippy blobs. The outline tape on the corrugated portable walls leaked paint everywhere.

Forget Banksy. It looked like a kindergartner had done it. A kindergartner doing stupid things to impress her hopefully-still-best-friend.

And how did I ever think painting a sign on a wall would convince Hrishi I was the same me? He'd liked me just fine the three years since his dare, with exactly zero Galactic Graffiti projects.

Only one thing had convinced me that had to change—one person.

Mackelle.

Mom could tell me to own my own choices all she wanted, but we might have to disagree on who started this.

"So why *did* you do it?" Mom's impatient voice broke through my freak-out.

"I don't know." I mumbled the words under my breath.

"What did you say?" she snapped, her forehead scrunching like this was causing her actual pain.

"I don't know!" My voice was sharp, too defensive. But her questions were needles on my skin.

"This is not a great time for you to get snippy with me. And it wasn't a great time for you to stop acting like yourself."

She was right. Trying to convince Hrishi I was the same old me, I did something totally *not* me.

He'd better not find out about this.

Mom wasn't finished. "I depend on you to be responsible. I've been fighting a migraine all day, I haven't slept well in a week, and I was finally starting to make progress on my post, when I get *this* phone call?"

Suddenly, I was filled with this white, hot anger. I couldn't quite tell if it was at her, at Mackelle, or maybe even at myself.

But it had to go somewhere, and Mom was the easiest target.

"I'm *sorry*."

"Well, you don't sound sorry."

I wasn't.

Not yet.

Chapter 34

AFTER

I haven't made it to the actual creek yet, still tromping over a hot, dry, sandy wash.

Once you reach the creek, this hike is magical, since walking in gentle current the whole way cools you off like nothing else could in the roasting desert sun. But for now, my sandals fill up every third step with sand, my face is dripping sweat, and already, my throat is gritty like it's made of sandstone.

I take a sip from Janie's hydration pack, but my tongue still sticks to the roof of my mouth. I'd better conserve, though. Eight miles is a long hike, and the creek water may be refreshing, but I can't drink it. Last year one of the rangers presented about microscopic life in Capitol Reef, and I can't unsee the slides of the wriggling Giardia parasite.

If Janie were here, she'd be whining about getting the adventure started.

Budge would ask how you spell "endless."

Dad would roll his eyes and tell us to keep walking.

Mom would check her GPS and tell Dad we've already been walking 2.2 miles, not one.

Right after my whole family helps me complain, I cross over

a swell of red earth and the ground ahead sparkles—a wide swath of rippling light.

Yes! The sound I thought was the slow, steady wind is actually the babbling water of Sulphur Creek.

"I did it!" I throw my arms wide as my voice echoes back from the canyon walls.

Oh.

Now that I can actually see Sulphur Creek, my steps slow.

I pause at the edge of the creek, hesitant to dip my toes into the chilly water. It looks deeper than I remembered—faster, and less clear. The murky, rusty water churns with red desert sand. The creek must still be flowing higher from the flood the day before yesterday.

I check the sky and comfort myself that with only a few wispy white clouds, rain isn't likely. Good thing, because it'll be nearly impossible to turn back once I start. And the three waterfalls aren't Niagara or anything, but the whole creek bed drops by twenty to thirty feet each time. And each time it does, I'll have to climb down with it—alone.

I squint against the bright sun glinting off the water, following the creek's path as far as I can see before it bends out of sight with the canyon wall.

This is my last chance to turn back, find Dad, and apologize for running off.

I shake my head slowly.

I'll see Dad, Janie, and Budge on the other side of this creek.

After I prove to them—and to myself—that I can be this brave.

I step forward, letting the cold water shock my hot, dusty toes, pulling at my calves in its hurry downstream.

So, we're really doing this? Mom's voice is more stunning than the frigid creek.

My eyes fly open as I spin to check if she's there, just over my shoulder—more Actual-Mom than Almost. For a fraction of a second it's like I can see her. Like she never left me.

But there's only red rocks, summer green cottonwoods, blue sky, sparkling water . . . and me.

I point my feet downstream in the chilly creek and walk purposefully forward. The current pulls me along, and I don't look back.

Chapter 35

BEFORE

Keilani Kahale <Keilanithegreat@mail.com>

To: Morgan Bell <soccermorgan4thewin@mail.com>

Subj: Graffiti-pocalypse

Sat, May 3 9:30 AM

Man. I don't know what to say.

I can't believe you got caught. I can't believe I didn't make you stop
before you started.

I'm sorry, Morgan. Epic friend-fail.
You grounded? My dad would probably ground me for a year. But your
mom's maybe cooler than my dad. Actually, forget maybe. She is. Way
cooler.

Anyway. You coming to Brianna's party? I hope so. But no worries if
you can't. It just won't be any fun without you, and I'll probably cry
in the corner with no one to practice synchronized swimming and
cannonballs with me.

—K

Letter Mom slipped under my bedroom door at ten, the morning after Graffiti-pocalypse:

Hey, Morgan,

So, that was rough last night, huh? I still don't understand why you did what you did, but it seems like you're hurting, and I'd like to understand a little better. You may not be ready to talk to me now, but I can wait.

In the meantime, I thought you might want to know I've done some out-of-character and inadvisable things to impress a boy myself.

(She knew. She *knew* this was about Hrishi. Also, "*out-of-character*" and "*inadvisable*"? Typical mom—super careful with her word choice. Dad would have just said "stupid")

There was this tall, handsome hiker man I met in college, as you know. And he was always doing these life-threatening acts of bravado

(Dad might have said "awesome" in this instance.)

—like hiking forever on minimal food with basically no rests. But I'm a sucker for a great set of shoulders and a strong jaw.

(*Eew.*)

Anyway, I told him I liked backpacking, even though my whole prior experience was hiking for an hour with a day pack at fifth-grade camp. Remind me to tell you the whole story, but you, Budge, and Janie are lucky you were ever born. I wasn't sure I'd make it.

(?!?!)

So while I don't know what's going on with Hrishi and Mackelle and Keilani, I do know from experience that these things are complicated. I'm here to help if you'll let me. And I know you'll figure it out. You're a pretty amazing kid, Morgan, and I'm proud of you. Always. Even when you do things that show a little less forethought than I'd like.

I think a Morgan-Mom date is a good idea. I'll finish my writing by noon. What do you say we go shopping for new bras, get lunch, and just talk?

(Now she was making me cry. I didn't deserve half this much niceness.)

Love you,
Mom

Mackelle Ryan <mackellebelle@mail.com>

To: Morgan Bell <soccermorgan4thewin@mail.com>

Subj: Get it!!

Sat, May 3 10:15 AM

Girl, that was amazing. I know you got caught, but not before you sent your message to your man. He's gonna love it. #WorthIt

(Seriously, what was *wrong* with her?)

Anyway. You coming to Brianna's party this afternoon? It's gonna be so fun but me and Keilani will be sad without our third musketeer.

(Triangle. That doesn't include you.)

(Also, no. I'm going out with my mom to try to fix the mess you made.)

(Okay, so . . . technically *I* made. But I still blame you. Gah!)

Plus, your favorite Jedi's going to be there.

(Oh, no.)

Haha. That's Hrishi, not Darth Vader or whoever. I made Brianna invite him just 4 U. So we can make sure he knows about your art.

(No!)

What can I say, I'm the best! ¯_(ツ)_/¯

(Nope. The actual worst.)

P.S. You have GOT to get a phone so we can text instead of email. Haha. Seriously. Ask your mom when she stops being mad.

(Mackelle is driving me crazy. Pushing me right around the bend.)

Chapter 36
AFTER

I round the first bend in the creek before Mom speaks again. *Not talking to me?*

I can't let myself. She's too real here. Every rock, sagebrush, and turn in the creek holds a memory.

Are you mad at me? I'm not the one who took off alone on a dangerous wilderness hike to prove a point, you know.

I growl, low in my throat. This wouldn't be dangerous if she were still alive, and we were here as a family.

Whoa. Maybe I should be glad you're not talking. You're in a mood.

"I am not in a mood." I slosh my angry feet through the water. *Okaaay.*

I stare into the murky water like my eyes will develop power to see through mud, but I'm stuck feeling my way over every rolling, moss-slippery rock in the creek bed.

Look up. You're missing one of the most beautiful trails on earth. If we're doing this, at least we should enjoy the view.

I take in the panorama of rippling canyon walls, sprinkled with pale green plants that poke up through red clay soil, with the shining ribbon of creek winding through it all.

I blink against the kind of beautiful that makes your eyes burn.

Real Mom should be here for this.

"*We* are not doing this," I say. "*I* am doing this. By myself. That's the whole point."

Wow. Sulky silent treatment followed by crabby answer. Teenagerhood is coming at us fast.

"Right. I'm mad because I'm twelve." I pick my way over large, rounded stones, barely visible above the swirling current.

So you are *mad.*

I don't answer. Because . . . duh.

Want to tell me why?

"I don't have to answer. You're not real."

You just did answer. And if I'm not real, why are you talking to me?

"Because you won't be quiet!" My savage cry echoes back to me from the high canyon walls.

Somewhere above there's a scenic overlook where people walk five feet from their cars, gaze down at the canyons, and take selfies looking like they went somewhere rugged and awesome.

I look up, shading my eyes with one hand, and check to see if tourists are looking down hundreds of feet, watching me yell at my imaginary mom.

That's not how you talked to me when I was alive.

Not usually. Only that one time. The memory churns inside me like the agitated creek.

"Right. Because you were alive. Which you're not now. So please—" Emotion chokes off my words.

At first, after I died, we used to have lemon drops. Her words are quiet, like the sound of the breeze through the canyon.

I clear my throat. "I stopped because it's too hard. Please, please, stop talking to me."

Just before the creek winds out of sight ahead, a single cottonwood grows out of the canyon floor. Its spreading branches grasp and reach, like it's searching for other trees that aren't there.

Maybe if I sit under its shade, both the tree and I will feel less alone for a little while. Besides, it's an ideal spot for a snack. My stomach rumbles in anticipation of whatever food Janie has stashed in her backpack.

My sandals squelch in fresh red mud, as I work my way over to the tree.

Mom's soft, worried voice stops me. *Where's your dad, Morgan? You really shouldn't be out here alone.*

I don't answer because she's right.

She's not real.

I am out here all alone.

My eyes sting from the bright sun, reflecting off the water, and suddenly I don't want to connect with a lonely tree.

I'll eat lunch at the first waterfall. It can't be far now.

I try to shake off the feeling that the tree is disappointed, watching me walk away.

Chapter 37

Mom was still in her office chair, fingers clacking over the keyboard, when I emerged from my room the morning after Morgan's Stupidest Decision Ever.

Now I had to go to Brianna's pool party instead of making things right with Mom, just to make sure Mackelle didn't send all the pieces of my life down Brianna's pool drain for her own entertainment.

As if she could sense my internal squirming, Mom looked up.

"Hey." She swiveled in her chair. Her too-tired eyes made me wonder how long she'd been up writing. But her smile was real.

Impossibly, she wasn't mad.

I dug my toes into the carpet, hoping I wasn't about to change that.

We both started talking at the same time.

"You got my note—"

"I'm sorry—"

Mom laughed. "Come here." She put her arms out, and I went in for a hug.

This was a constant. Mom might get mad. She might get

disappointed. But she was—as she was always telling me—team Morgan for life.

I wanted to stay like that, wrapped in her forgiving arms, but I had to ask about the party.

I pulled away so I could see her face.

"Mom?"

"Yeah."

"The Morgan-Mom date sounds awesome. I really want to do it."

"Great. I'll be ready in a couple more hours. Can you do your chores?"

I took a deep breath. "It's just . . ."

She cocked her head at me.

"Well . . . am I grounded?"

"Have you ever been grounded?" Her one raised eyebrow asked if I knew her at all.

"No, but after yesterday, I thought . . ."

She shook her head. "Not a big fan of grounding. Too arbitrary. Natural consequences, though? Fixing your own messes? That's my jam. Like when the school gets back to us about payment for damages, you'll have plenty to deal with, making things right."

Wow. Natural consequences fell like a cloak of doom over my shoulders.

"But how will I pay to repaint a portable? I don't even have a job."

"You can do a lot of things when you have no other choice,"

Mom said brightly. "Maybe on our date today I can help you come up with a solid ABC plan to take care of things?"

A surge of anger heated my face.

Keilani was wrong. My mom wasn't cooler than her dad. Just smarter. In a diabolical way—like inside her head, she was drumming the tips of her fingers together and cackling.

No, I won't punish you. I'll use words like "natural consequences," and "owning your own choices," then help you ABC plan your own punishment.

Even as I set my teeth and folded my arms across my chest, I knew I had no right to be angry. But I couldn't stop myself.

"Great, so if I'm not grounded, then I can go to Brianna's party this afternoon." I didn't try to smooth the rough edge in my voice.

Mom leaned back, looking me up and down like she was just now seeing me.

She nodded slowly like she could read my angry thoughts. "So . . . no Morgan-Mom date?"

"That's what I was coming to tell you." I looked down at my folded arms, trying too late to lighten my tone. "I already promised I'd be there today."

I could be purposeful about my word choice too. Mom was big on keeping one's word.

"But we should totally go another time," I said. "I do need the new bra."

Mom massaged around her collar bone, her lips twisting like I'd hurt her.

"And talking too," I said quickly. "You're right. We should talk. Maybe tonight?"

She looked at me for a long second, then let out a long sigh that seemed to shrink her.

"Maybe it's better anyway. I haven't been sleeping well this week, and I'm feeling a bit off today too. Can you be home in time for dinner? I'm making your favorite—spaghetti."

"Yeah." I felt wrong, wrong inside, even though she'd agreed to what I wanted. "I'll see you tonight. Then after dinner we'll talk. Promise."

Chapter 38

AFTER

The sun beats down from directly overhead, and my feet ache like I've come miles already. The rushing creek grows louder—drowning out any sound Mom could make, even if she wanted to talk.

Thankfully, she's gone quiet.

I come around the next bend in the canyon, and stop, because now I know I *have* come miles.

The creek was amplified by the first waterfall—flowing faster and fuller than I've ever seen it—Mini-Niagara.

Okay, very mini. But still, watching that much water roar over the edge and plummet down to the rocky creek bed below makes me dizzy.

I slosh over to the bank, fighting the creek every step, and collapse on the sun-warmed sandstone to rest my battered, pruney feet. Then I dig into Janie's Hiking Survival Backpack for lunch.

The first three things I find do not inspire hope in Janie's survival skills. Especially since I'm hungry enough to eat my own arm.

1. The stuffed skunk she got in her Easter basket, first named Flora, then Rainbow Sparkle, and now . . . Lily?

2. The pink washcloth Janie uses to swaddle Flora-Rainbow-Sparkle-Lily.

3. An empty lip balm tube. For . . . uh . . . pretending to put on lip balm?

Great. Now my lips feel raw and chafed too.

The fourth thing makes my stomach feel like I just jumped over that waterfall.

Lemon drops. A whole baggie, full to bursting.

Of course Janie prepared herself a personal stash. She loves them for all the reasons. The sour, the sweet, and the excuse to talk with a captive audience.

But seriously, Universe? *Lemon drops?*

I shove them into a side pocket, where I won't have to look at them, and keep searching for food.

I find two granola bars, one battered and squishy apple, and seven—holy hoarder, Janie—packets of fruit snacks. I tear through a bar and two bags of gummies like they're my only hope of avoiding self-cannibalism.

My stomach still feels floppy-hollow around my "lunch." But I take a swig of water to fill in the gaps, leaving the rest of the food for later. I'm pretty sure the first waterfall is the halfway mark, and that's a lot of walking left to do on one gross apple, a granola bar, and five packs of fruit snacks.

Note to self: educate Janie on the definition of the word "survival."

So it's Janie's fault? Who decided to hike alone with zero preparation?

I choke on a mouthful of granola bar. "Seriously? You say nothing for like two miles, but now you'll pipe up to tell me I'm wrong?"

Why am I surprised? That was Mom. All about owning our own choices.

Fair enough. Her voice holds stifled laughter. *What should we talk about besides your current wrongness?*

My words well up—pressurized like the fizz in a bottle of soda, all set to explode when you loosen the lid.

And suddenly I realize it's not just now. I've been mad at Mom for a while. Missing her, yeah. Every day. But also so, so angry.

I shove the stupid stuffed skunk and her pink blankie and the useless lip balm back into Janie's pack. I'd have less weight without them, but Janie would kill me if I ditched them, and Dad has trained me to feel the same way about litter as I do about best-friend-stealing drama queens.

I stand up and sling my pack over my shoulder.

Break time is over. I've got to finish this hike, starting with climbing down around this waterfall.

You can talk to me, Mom says quietly. *I'm here.*

"Not really." I edge forward on the overhang so I can see the precarious path to the canyon floor below. "So, what's the point?"

I inch along the narrow lip where the sandstone bulges out.

The footholds are barely there, and below, the creek gushes down twenty feet into an unforgiving stone bowl.

I can't even watch this.

"Shh." I don't need Mom's heights-anxiety splitting my focus as I turn my back to the falls, leaning my weight into my arms and away from my feet, pressing the soles of my shoes flat against the rock like Dad taught me.

I can't believe your dad ever got me to do this hike the first time.

"You loved it," I grunt, reaching to grip a small handhold in the rock above me.

I remember her at the bottom of this exact waterfall, one hand on her lower back and one hand shielding her eyes from the bright sky, as she grinned back up at the top of the falls—joyful.

I loved having climbed it. Not the climbing of it so much.

I get that. Right now, I'm at the spot where I'd reach out for Dad's hand to stabilize me. The footholds are like knuckle bumps, and handholds barely exist.

I feel my arms and legs start to shake, my chest tightening painfully, but a panic attack right now would be a disaster. So, I hold very still, try to match my breathing with the steady, lulling sound of the water.

Morgan?

"Stop talking." The words squeeze out through my clenched teeth. "I have to concentrate, and you. Are. Not. Here."

I'm as here as I can be.

"It's not enough."

I ease forward, every part of me coiled tight as a spring, until

I can swing my left foot onto a solid base. Then I guide myself gently over the lip of the rock, ballet-pointing one foot until it touches the ledge below, and using my shaking arms to ease myself down. From there, it's just a few careful steps before I can slide down the sharply angled sandstone to the canyon floor.

Good job, Morgan! The pride in Mom's voice makes me smile as I drop to the ground.

But instead of hitting dry sand like always, I splash into knee-deep muddy water. The creek has overflowed its bed.

This is new.

"Yeah." And not good new. New like Mackelle, hanging constantly with me and Keilani, playing *my* soccer position.

The canyon walls above us look wet, but waterfall spray doesn't reach this far. I reach a hand to the moist, cold sandstone, and my fingers come away coated in red mud.

If there's mud this high, then—

I gasp when I see what's ahead.

At least five feet above me, a smooth log—wider than me around and longer than Dad—is wedged sideways between the canyon walls.

At its ends, snugged tight against the sandstone, limp tangles of desert grass, reeds, and branches hang, caught like the hair that twists around our vacuum cleaner brush.

Yesterday's flood pushed a giant log through the canyon with enough force to jam it into that tight space, leaving it as a warning to future hikers. That same flood left wet mud above my head in a place where there's usually no creek at all.

Morgan. Mom says my name like a warning.

Visions of surging water take my breath away.

What if we'd been hiking together when the flood surged through here?

And what if it rains again today, with the creek already so high?

I peer up through the gap in the narrow canyon walls at the slim ribbon of visible blue sky, dolloped with clouds like white scoops of mashed potato on a blue plate. Janie would say they're cumulus, not rain clouds—which should be comforting. But there are a lot more than when I started.

There'd better not be more coming. Because as I look back up at the waterfall, roaring endlessly behind me, and at the steep route I climbed down, I know I couldn't go back if I wanted to.

It's okay. We've got this, Mom says in her forced-optimistic let's-ABC-plan-our-way-out voice. Like she can save me if it does start raining. If the river rises.

If . . . anything at all.

I can feel her behind me, like she's about to put her arm around me.

Tears burn my eyes at the thought of the hug I can't have. Not now. Not ever.

Let me help.

"You can't," I say. "No one can. I can only help myself."

Chapter 39

BEFORE

I rode my bike to Brianna's party. Mom wasn't feeling well, and I wasn't about to ask Hrishi for a ride. Before I saw him, I had to make sure Keilani and Mackelle hadn't talked to him, and weren't about to.

Hrishi and I lived on a quiet street, our houses so close together I could smell the Rogan Josh simmering in Mrs. Patel's kitchen from our back porch, so I always knew when it was a good time to "drop by." So close Hrishi could hear every bellow from Budge when Mom made him leave the trampoline for chores, so he knew when to stay away.

But Brianna lived in a gated community on the hill, with strategically placed ornamental trees that hid her neighbors tidily from view. Her dad was an orthodontist. And, boy . . . straightening smiles must pay well. Her house was on a lot so wide it could have held four the size of mine and Hrishi's.

I rode my bike down the long driveway, propped it against the third garage, swung open the wrought iron gate, and followed the sounds of laughter and splashing to the backyard pool.

At least thirty kids from school were swimming, playing

water volleyball, or lounging around the deck. I searched first for Hrishi, but didn't spot him anywhere.

Perfect. I could catch Mackelle and Keilani before he even showed up.

"Morgan!" Brianna hurried over in a retro red terry cloth cover-up. "Yay! You're in time for the diving competition."

"Thanks." I eyed the high dive warily. I might be coordinated on the soccer field, but my dives were about as graceful as a hippo's belly flop.

"Keilani!" I waved to get her attention, and she swam to my side of the pool.

"You're here!" She beamed. "I worried you were grounded after all."

I shook my head, putting a finger to my lips. I wished she hadn't mentioned grounding, out loud where anyone could hear. Did people already know what I'd done?

My heartbeat pulsed from my scalp to my fingertips as I scanned the crowd for one particular head of dark hair.

I leaned down by the pool. "Is *he* here?"

But Mackelle reached the side of the pool then, and she answered first. "Not yet!" she bubbled. "But this is sooo exciting." She pushed out of the water in one fluid motion, swiveling her hips to sit on the edge of the pool. Her long brown hair hung over one shoulder in a sleek ponytail.

Even dripping wet, she looked put together.

"Shh." I looked around. "Can you guys come out here? We need to talk."

"Oooh." Mackelle helped Keilani out of the pool, and they both grabbed their towels.

"You okay?" Keilani asked.

"Of course she's okay," Mackelle squealed. "She's more than okay." She put two cold, clammy hands on my shoulders. "Spill," she said dramatically. "All. The. Tea."

"Stop." I glanced around again. "That's what I'm trying to tell you. There is no tea. And I need you to get it."

Brianna wheeled out her parents' giant Bluetooth speaker and microphone. "Testing, testing. Is this thing on? It's time for our diving competition," she said in a game show host voice.

"I'm in lots of trouble," I hissed. "It was totally stupid, and I . . . just really wish I hadn't done it."

"Come on, it was brillia—"

"No," I snapped. "And I need you to—"

"Participants line up by the diving board," Brianna continued. "Points will be awarded for originality, daring, and aesthetic appeal. With a fabulous prize for the winner. Remember Jeff Parks, winning with his triple flip last year?"

She grinned at me. "And we're thrilled to have last August's Disaster Dive winner here today—Morgan Bell, ladies and gentlemen. After her . . . er . . . magnificent cartwheel-flop last year, we're excited to see what she'll try today."

I slapped my palm to my forehead. I did not need more attention right now.

"Wait. Morgan and I were cowinners of the Disaster Dive," Keilani said. "My cannonball blew the judges away."

"You both made quite a *splash*." Brianna winked.

"Of course Keilani made a splash," Mackelle whispered, cupping her hands in front of her, miming large boobs and snorting with laughter.

A couple of boys in the pool started snickering, and the tips of Keilani's ears turned pink.

"Come on." Keilani linked her arm through mine, pulling me toward the diving board. Me and Keilani linking arms and turning our backs on Mackelle was a move in the right direction.

"Lani, wait!" Mackelle squealed as she hurried to join us in line. "You know I'm jealous. Don't be mad." She pouted up at Keilani.

"Maybe think before you say things," I snapped.

Keilani stopped me with a hand on my arm. "It's okay."

"Blabbing can make things worse. Which is why I need you both to be cool about Hrishi."

"I'm *always* cool." Mackelle huffed. "I'm just glad I'm going to be here when you see his reaction. It'll be like—" Her jaw dropped and her eyes sparkled. I thought she was imitating his future expression until—

"Hey, guys," Hrishi's voice said from right behind me. Warm and scratchy and . . . just—Hrishi. Goose bumps popped out all over my arms and legs.

"You're here." I turned, determined to act normal. But my face burned all the way to my hairline.

"So are you." He grinned. "But you might as well leave. Because I'm gonna parkour off the diving board. None of you stand a chance." He kicked my flip-flops like always, and my stomach did a flip-flop of its own. He definitely didn't know yet, and I needed to keep it that way.

"*Hri-shi*," Mackelle sang. "How's it *go-ing*?"

He shook his head, looking baffled as usual around Mackelle. "Uh . . . good?"

"Have you been by the school today?" Mackelle cocked her head at him, her expression all meaningful, and I elbowed her arm. *This* was being cool?

"It's Saturday." Hrishi wrinkled his nose at her.

"I know, but—"

"Mackelle!" I yelled. "Let's get some soda. Now."

Her eyes went wide, and then she cackled like she was trying out for the role of the witch in *Wicked*.

"Oh my goodness, Morgan." Mackelle pity-pouted her lips again. "Mackelle is going to do you a big, huge favor. You, too, Hrishi." She beelined for Brianna and her microphone.

"Mackelle!" I called.

"What's going on?" Hrishi asked.

"Before the contest begins," Mackelle said into the mic, "I have an announcement."

No!

I started toward her.

"Yesterday Morgan became a great local artist."

"Mackelle!"

"I don't know if any of you have seen her mural yet, but it's a special message for someone she cares about sooo much."

I started running.

"Everyone should check out the sweet painting she did on the side of the sixth-grade portable. She got in trouble, but it was so worth it to finally show Hrish—Aaaah!"

Mackelle and I were not on the same team today, and there were no red cards in pool parties. I flew into her with so much force that she staggered back a few steps, and then I tripped on the microphone cord, shoving her into the pool, and flying right in after her.

It was Disaster Dive gold medal material.

When we came gasping to the surface, everyone was talking, pointing.

Staring.

Hrishi's eyes were widest of all—glued to my face like he'd never seen me before.

Chapter 40

AFTER

Mom doesn't stop talking for the next thirty minutes—relentless, exactly like when she was alive.

I can't believe we made it over that waterfall.

You giving me the silent treatment? You do realize this little adventure was your decision?

I stomp angrily through the creek, splash-soaking the hem of my shorts, and slapping at the cattails growing taller than me at the edge of the creek bed.

If I don't respond, she'll go away.

That was my theory anyway. Early test results are not promising.

You're definitely bottling up some feelings, here. Let's take a break, Morgan. Talk, maybe?

What we need is to keep moving. According to my phone, it's already three o'clock. Dad must be freaking out.

The canyon walls narrow, and the water's roar builds, echoing around me in the tight chamber. I must be almost to the second waterfall—which I will figure out how to cross, even though I don't remember how we did it last time.

Come on, Morgan. Talk to me.

Ignore. Breathe. Ignore. Breathe. One careful step at a time.

It's just, you don't seem happy.

It's this—the most obvious statement ever—that finally breaks my vow of silence.

"I'm not!" I snap. "How am I supposed to be happy?"

Do you want to be happy?

Oh, no.

No, no. No.

She is *not* dragging me into one of her self-help conversations, trying to fix me like one of her clients.

"No, Mom. I despise happiness."

Stomp. Splash. Stomp. Splash.

"That's why I'm making myself and Dad and everyone else miserable."

You know, Morgan. As communication tools go, sarcasm is not very—

I let out a primal cry of rage, stopping still to fight the current. "I'm not trying to use powerful communication tools, Mom. And I don't need you to positive-psychology me so I can harness my personal resilience. I'm only talking to fake-you because you won't stop talking in my head."

My heart pounds so hard in my chest, I double over, bracing my hands on my thighs as I gasp in air. I can see the second waterfall now—the creek rushing toward a narrow funnel where it plunges over the cliff ahead. The water pulls so hard—one slip and it could suck me into the torrent and hurl me over the falls.

Ohh. It's a heartbroken sound. *Sweet Morgan Beth. Hurting so badly.*

Her words are what's hurting.

"Stop." I struggle to the bank, dragging myself on hands and knees onto the steep, rocky embankment to the right of the falls. "Stop talking to me."

But, sweetheart, you'll only make it worse, pushing people away.

My face floods with heat, legs shaking like I just played mid-field for two forty-five-minute halves.

"I can't make it worse than you already made it." Hot tears sting my eyes. "You promised, Mom. You promised me." A sob rises in my throat, making me choke on my words. "How could you break a promise like that?"

Chapter 41

BEFORE

My legs and lungs burned as I pedaled the two miles from Brianna's mansion to my house. But I wasn't jealous anymore of Brianna and her pool and her humongous yard and invisible neighbors. Although maybe I would be when I woke up tomorrow and Hrishi was still my neighbor.

I'd rather hide from him for the rest of my life.

But my house had one thing Brianna's could never have—Mom.

I knew from years of experience that if I could just talk to her it would all be okay.

It wouldn't matter that I blew off our mother-daughter date for a stupid party where I only made a bad situation worse.

It wouldn't matter that I made Morgan's Stupidest Decision Ever to impress a boy, and now I couldn't look one of my two best friends in the eye.

I shuddered, picturing the shocked look on Hrishi's face. Stupid, nosy Mackelle probably made up the whole thing about him wanting me to notice him.

At least I knew Mom would stop everything for a lemon

drop, and after I let out all the junk I'd been holding in, somehow everything would be better.

I hopped off my bike, letting it clatter in a heap in the middle of the lawn, and ran into the house.

"Mom!"

"In the kitchen."

She was stirring spaghetti on the stove, wearing jeans and a bright purple tee shirt, with her hair up in a messy ponytail.

The sight of her calmly making dinner brought tears to my eyes.

"Mom."

"Morgan?"

She turned toward me, took one look at my face, and her eyes widened in concern. Two long steps and I was in the safe circle of her arms, right where I fit, with my face against her neck. I could feel the quick flutter of her pulse against my forehead.

"Sweetheart?"

I couldn't talk, I was crying so hard.

"Morgan." Her hand stroked the back of my hair as her chest rose and fell in short, shallow breaths. "Oh, baby girl. Sweet Morgan Beth. It's all right. It'll be okay. I promise."

"Oh, Mom." I pulled away to look into her face. "I messed everything up so bad."

I cried in her arms for a minute or two, whispering all the dumb, Morgan-caused chaos, while she murmured comfort into my hair.

"I know it's nothing you can't fix," she said. "Hold on. You can tell me everything. I just need . . . I think I need to sit down a minute." She swayed on her feet, steadying herself with a hand on the counter.

"Mom?"

"One second. I need to . . . catch my breath." Her voice was airy, faint.

"Are you okay?"

"I'm going to sit down for a second. So dizzy." She leaned against the counter, her legs folding under her as she eased herself onto the floor.

 Fear clamped a hand around my chest.

"Haha. I guess I'm sitting here." Dark circles under her eyes stood out against her pale face.

"Where's Dad?" I said. "Janie," I called. "Get Dad."

"He's. Still. At work." Mom's words puffed out between straining breaths.

The room swirled around me, like her dizziness was catching.

"I'm . . . sorry, sweetheart." Mom put her hand over her heart as I fell to my knees beside her. "We'll need . . . to talk . . . later. I think something's wrong. You should . . . call 9-1-1."

I called.

Paramedics were there in five minutes, but it felt like a hundred.

Then it was chaos. Stethoscopes and blood pressure cuffs, barked orders into radios, and a team moving Mom carefully onto a stretcher.

And all that time I couldn't do anything.

Not until they were wheeling her out to the ambulance, when I heard her call my name, and I rushed to be with her, Budge and Janie running after, crying.

"I'll see you again so soon," Mom said, as loud as she could with her voice all turned to wisps of breath. "I'll be okay. Promise. Then we can talk about everything. And you'll be okay too."

Hot tears blurred my view of her face.

She looked at Budge and Janie, hurrying to keep up with us, then up at me.

Between gasps for air, she whispered, "Keep them safe, Morgan. Be brave for them. Help them be happy."

"I promise."

Dad made it home twenty minutes after the ambulance took her away.

On the way to the hospital, his car zoomed faster through the pink-tinged sunset streets than I'd ever seen him drive before. "She's okay," I said for like the tenth time. "We'll see her when we get there. She promised me. And Mom always keeps her promises."

"I'm sure you're right," Dad said in a voice as tight as his grip on the steering wheel. "I'm sure she'll be fine."

Chapter 42

AFTER

I stagger on jelly legs to look over the second waterfall. The creek roars down, down, down into the rocky trench it has carved below. There has to be a way over, since the other times we hiked here we weren't forced to stop and build a permanent home, but to my right the steep embankment shows no possible path. The other bank is a sheer drop-off. I have no memory of how we got down last time.

Don't stop talking to me now, Mom says.

I shake my head. I need to think—find a way over.

Don't shut me out, she pleads. *What's been the hardest part?*

"You want to know the hardest part?" I yell, scanning the rocky falls for any hint of a path down. "It's Plan B—forever. And I hate Plan B! I hate it every minute of every day. Plan B is no more soccer. No free time. No clothes that fit. Not even a real bra. Holy cow, Mom, I can't start seventh grade without a real bra—you said so!" A weird laugh-sob bursts out as I scrape my knees over the rough sandstone, climbing the steep embankment to my right for a better view.

A weird laugh-sob bursts out as I scrape my knees over the rough sandstone, climbing the steep embankment to my right for a better view. It's weird to go on about soccer and bras, when they're not even close to the most important thing I'm missing. But it's just easier to fixate on underwear and sports instead of the gaping hole in my chest that feels like a permanent part of me.

"Plan B equals no friends. Keilani isn't even talking to me anymore," I choke out. "And I was so embarrassed I couldn't look at Hrishi before he went away."

On my knees, I grip sagebrush branches with both hands to help pull myself to the top of the rise, scraping my palms as I go.

"Plan B equals no one to talk to. No more lemon drops. No one to help me figure out all the stuff only you could understand. No late night back rubs when I'm freaking out about everything. It equals—"

Tears flow freely down my face, sting my throat, try to choke my words, but I can't stop now.

"Plan B equals—" The words scrape over my throat, burning on their way out. "No you."

The wind blows hard and fast, and I rub my arms, fighting the chill.

"Don't tell me to make the best of Plan B, Mom. Plan B is what's left after Plan A leaves you. Then trying to prove you can handle Plan B, you blow right past it to Plan C, and pretty soon you're at Plan D: DISASTER." I stagger to my feet, balling my stinging hands into fists at my side. "Because Plan A is dead—forever!"

Mom doesn't say anything. I told her not to, so it shouldn't make me feel so alone.

"And if Plan A is dead, that means you can't help me find my way past this waterfall, right?" I wrap my arms around myself, holding on tight. "You can't give me advice about my best friends, or even give me a hug."

Silence.

"Can you?" I need to hear her answer.

No. Her voice is quiet, like she's farther away than she was a minute before.

"No," I echo. "You could, if you were still here. You promised you'd stay, but it wasn't true."

Silence.

I can still feel her here, but there's nothing she can say.

"I wish it was true." Sobs shake my shoulders. "I wish you dying was a bad dream and I could wake up. But I can't, so . . ." The words stick in my throat, but I have to do the rest of this hike on my own—one hundred percent by myself. So I force them out, quiet but firm. "I need you to go now and let me do this by myself. Okay?"

I stare up into the sky—too bright, even with the gathering clouds. So bright that when I blink, behind my eyelids there's blinding white. Then I hear the barest hint of a whisper over the rushing waterfall.

Okay.

And just like that . . .

She's gone.

Chapter 43

BEFORE

White:

Dad's knuckles on the steering wheel.

The sign: Mountain Star Hospital

The papers on the check-in desk.

Bright, cold, sterile white:

Cinder block walls.

Fluorescent lights, buzzing in the too-quiet waiting room.

Coat on the tall, thin doctor with the veiny hands.

"I'm sorry." The doctor's voice was low, serious. "I'm so sorry."

Dad's face, as he slumped back into his chair—pale, sagging white.

"Where's Mom?" Budge's voice was shrill.

"We did all we could," the doctor said. "It was a pulmonary embolism. Multiple large clots in both lungs."

We did all we could? My heart forgot how to beat.

"Where's Mom?" Janie's voice whispered at my side.

The doctor in the white coat glanced down at me and Budge

and Janie, then back up at Dad. His eyes were very old and very sad as he asked his question. "Mr. Bell, would you like to see her body? I could have a nurse wait with the children."

Not her. *Her body.*

And they were going to take just Dad. Leave us here?

"Dad," I whispered, begging with my eyes. "I have to see her."

"*We* have to," Janie corrected me, her voice so small.

"We'll go together," Dad said, his colorless lips barely moving.

He carried Budge.

Janie's hand was so small, finding mine. I couldn't look at her.

All I could see was white:

Linoleum floor.

Ceiling tiles.

Blanket covering the body lying still, still, still on the bed.

The doctor gently peeled back the sheet, and Dad's face crumpled into a new, broken shape, as he reached out to hold Mom's too-white hand in his.

I stayed frozen where I was.

Her brown hair spilled dark across the white bed sheet.

Her hair looked familiar, but her face didn't.

Her face was the pale wax mask of someone who wasn't— could never be—my mom.

My mom, who'd promised she'd see me later that night, but wouldn't see me ever again.

Chapter 44

AFTER

I'm still shaking, tears still wet on my cheeks from sending Mom away. But the sun has dipped behind the clouds, which are definitely thicker than even half an hour ago.

I can't wait. I've got to find a way over.

If Janie were here, she'd hug me and thank me for the most awesome adventure yet.

Dad would probably say something like, "This is easy. We've totally got this." Unless he opted for "What were you thinking?" or, "You're grounded forever."

Budge would say, "It's like *Paper Mario*, Morgan. There's always a solution. Let me try."

Budge isn't wrong. I've been here before. There has to be a way. In *Paper Mario*, it's about shifting your perspective, flipping to 3-D mode to discover paths you couldn't see before.

From here, the only place to get a different perspective is to climb higher.

My feet slip in the sandy soil as I scramble to the top of the next rise, gripping rough sage branches for support. From up here, I see a seam in the rock running parallel to the waterfall, dropping down and out of sight.

A hysterical laugh bursts through my lips. I found it—by myself.

The seam is filled with boulders that look sturdy enough to be climbable. Even though it twists out of my view, I have a strong memory of lowering my body through a tight space like this, with Dad waiting below to cushion my fall.

I grip the rocks with trembling fingers, borrowing some of their steadiness.

I can do this.

Mom always said you can do a lot of things when you have no other choice.

I use my feet on either side of the tight space to bridge my way down. Then holding most of my weight with my arms, I slowly lower myself.

I can't see what lies below, so I have to reach, sliding myself gently down and hoping I'll find a stable foothold.

I'm stretching into the darkness, shaking with the effort of holding my body weight, when my arms give out, and I fall hard.

My ankle turns as I land and a sharp pain shoots halfway up my leg.

I crumple in a ball on the rocky canyon floor.

Chapter 45

THE WEEK AFTER

When Keilani's grandma was dying two years ago, she told her family, "Don't you put me in a box in a church and make people come stand around crying while they stare at me. Spread my ashes in the sea, and roast the biggest pig you can find to celebrate my going home."

When you died young and quick like Mom did, there was no time to ask what you wanted. And Mom, who had a plan for everything, had no plan for her own funeral.

So we put her body in a box in a church, and people came to cry and stare. Her adoring fans and clients sent more flowers than I'd ever seen in one place. If I never see another giant floral arrangement, that'll be great with me.

I stood by Dad. Budge and Janie stood by me. We wore dark colors and tried not to cry while people watched us. Dad's eyes were already glazed and shadowed with The Fog, so he didn't really see anyone. Not Grandma Bell, who went back and forth helping and arranging quietly in the background. Not the dozens of Mom's in-person clients who came to grieve over losing their life coach. Not even me and Budge and Janie.

Most of the people were just dark clothes, blurry faces—all saying the same words over and over.

"Your mom changed my life."

"She was the most amazing woman."

"So sorry for your loss."

"If there's anything I can do . . ."

And the ones I hated most of all: "She's in a better place."

Keilani and Tama came through with their mom and dad—huddled close together like they still belonged together. They wore colorful leis and island prints. Keilani's sky blue dress had white palm fronds and hibiscus flowers splashed across the fabric.

Her eyes were red, like she'd been crying for days. But looking at her made me feel like I'd start, and if I started, I knew it would be days for me too.

I stared instead at her brown sandals so I wouldn't have to see her face, while she hugged me quick and hard.

"Thank you for coming." Today, that was my family's version of "Sorry for your loss" and "If there's anything I can do . . ."

Keilani's family moved on, and for a second, I thought of going with her. Finding a plate of funeral sandwiches, hiding out behind a potted tree in the lobby where we could both say nothing for as long as we wanted. But before I found the courage, another faceless woman in black was tearing up as she apologized for my loss.

I thanked her for coming.

Hrishi wore a suit.

A *suit.*

He pulled at the collar with one finger, and stood tucked slightly behind his mom like he was hiding from me.

I kept waiting for him to walk over and kick the shiny, black toes of my funeral shoes with the white toes of his Converse, so I would know that whatever had happened, we were still good. Still . . . us. But when I caught his eye, he just nodded, his face a too-serious Hrishi mask.

After he and his family left, I told Dad I needed the restroom. It didn't seem like he even noticed when I went missing for twenty minutes.

Hrishi not kicking my feet, of all things, was the only part of the funeral that made me cry.

Chapter 46
AFTER

"It's okay," I murmur to myself, trying not to cry, curled up on the hard canyon floor. The fear that I won't be able to walk—that I'll be trapped out here alone—hurts nearly as bad as my ankle.

I push up onto hands and knees, moving slowly to stand on my left foot. I take one step, and searing pain makes my right ankle threaten to give out. I wince, trying to hold all my weight with my left.

I shake my head to clear it. I've got to think, be logical.

If I hurt myself at soccer, we'd ice it. Maybe cool creek water will help the swelling.

Using a boulder to stabilize myself, I hop to the edge of the creek and immerse my foot. I sigh as the chill water brings immediate relief.

I dig through Janie's backpack again, looking for anything I can use.

I still have to finish the hike on my own. Have to. Anything else proves Dad right—that I'm far too broken to trust with a task like the one Mom gave me. Far too lost to be brave for our family, let alone to keep anyone safe or happy.

So it's probably a good thing I can't use Mom's phone to call for help. It can't tempt me anyway, since without coverage, it's basically just a judgy clock, reminding me every time I check it how quickly time is passing.

But Janie's supplies aren't much help. Why couldn't she have swaddled her pet skunk in a tension bandage, or brought ibuprofen instead of lemon drops?

Then again, Dad always says when you're in the wilderness, you work with what you've got.

I loosen my sandal, roll up the pink washcloth, and wrap it as tight as I can around my ankle. Then I cinch my sandal strap over the rag splint to hold it snug.

I wish I could rest, but I don't like the look of the sky. Now instead of scoops of mashed potatoes on a blue plate, it looks more like shards of blue plate on a bed of mashed potatoes.

It can't rain while I'm in this canyon.

I brace myself against the rocks, pushing myself to stand. My heartbeat keeps time with my throbbing ankle as I take a tentative step with my right foot.

It still hurts—bad. But whether it's the cloth or the soak in cold water, it's a bit more bearable.

I can walk. My whole body is a sigh of relief.

I limp along, keeping out of the current whenever I can, scanning the bank for a driftwood walking stick. Every step over rolling rocks in churning brown water, I risk hurting my ankle worse, making it impossible to finish the hike. Possibly putting myself in real danger.

I shake my hands like Alejandro showed me, like I'm physically throwing away the too-heavy thought.

Every step I take, the canyon narrows, and the water deepens.

When it reaches my waist, I slip off my pack, holding it above my head as I move slowly deeper. I can't risk soaking it. Mom's phone is in there.

On my next step, my foot barely brushes the soft, sandy bottom, and I slip, gasping in a silty mouthful of creek water as my head goes under. I flail to the surface, swimming a few yards before my feet connect with the creek bed again.

I stagger out of the surprise pool, each step shooting pain through my ankle.

My backpack is soaked. Mom's phone!

Please, please don't be wet. Don't be broken.

I fumble with pack's drenched zipper as I limp to the bank, which feels nothing like solid land. The clay mud tries to suck me in with each step.

I find a rock that isn't slick with fresh mud and slump, shivering miserably in my soaked clothes.

I pull out the phone with trembling fingers and remove the damp case, wiping water droplets away with my fingers. Everything I could use to dry it is sopping with muddy water.

I press the power button and the screen flares immediately to life.

Relief turns my stomach to Jell-O. My plan, all Mom's phone pics and apps that I mostly haven't had the courage to look at—they're still there.

On the lock screen, the exclamation point icon reminds me that there's no service in the middle of the wilderness. Underneath, there's a pic of me, Janie, and Budge, sitting on our front porch on the first day of school. Mom took the photo, laughing behind the camera, begging Budge to hold still for one second so she could capture the moment.

Wishing I hadn't sent her away so quickly, I scroll through the images, hungry for her smile, her eyes that would see me, know me.

But Mom wasn't much of a selfie person, always behind the camera. As I swipe from photo to photo, I find Janie jumping up and down on her seventh birthday with her new big-girl Hiking Survival Backpack. Me, in my soccer uniform, grinning after the Rocky Mountain win. Budge hanging from the monkey bars.

I pause on a photo I forgot all about—Me and Hrishi and Keilani together in our backyard. We were grinning our heads off, standing arm in arm in front of our peach tree, all glowy with pink spring blossoms. Hard to believe that was only a few months ago—so much has changed.

I keep scrolling, searching, and finding no Mom—until I reach the video files.

And there she sits, in a bright purple tee shirt, her hair in a ponytail, sitting in front of her ACTION, BACKUP, CLEANUP video background. It's not a still, lifeless picture.

A video clip.

Of Mom.

Talking with her own voice, her own mannerisms.

I push play, and hold my breath, waiting for her to speak.

"Hey, guys." She smiles at the camera. "This is Eve Bell with episode forty-three of ACTION, BACKUP, CLEANUP. Today I'm doing something a little different. Sometimes I do viewer shout-outs on this channel, but this weekend . . ." She purses her lips, looking up at the ceiling like she always did when she was searching for words.

I cradle the phone in my hand.

"This weekend was a rough one. My twelve-year-old daughter made some uncharacteristically foolish choices."

Foolish choices? When did I—

"And then we argued," Mom says. "And she's still not ready to talk to me."

Shivers of realization tingle over my skin. We almost never argued. We discussed, disagreed. But unless you count baby tantrums, in my whole life I can only remember one fight—the day before Mom died.

I pause the video, memory flooding my mind.

That shirt she's wearing—bright purple, a stark contrast with her too-pale skin, with the ivory linoleum, as she lay on the floor and I counted her breaths while we waited for the ambulance.

Mom recorded this video on May third.

I need two of Alejandro's four-four-eight breaths before I can press play again.

"And I'm in favor of waiting to talk until you've had space to figure things out for yourself," Mom says with a sad smile. "But in the meantime, I have some things I need to say, and I think they'll be helpful to the general audience of this channel. So, I hope you'll indulge me as I record this video as a message to my twelve-year-old daughter—Morgan."

Mom recorded a video message to *me* the day she died?

Pause.

Inhale, two, three, four.

Hold, two, three, four.

Exhale, two, three, four, five, six, seven, eight.

I lean closer to the phone like I can climb inside the video.

"So, Morgan Beth." Mom looks straight into my eyes, now burning with unshed tears. "You were pretty mad at me this morning. Basically, the second I brought up the ABC planning. Which is nothing new, I know." She shakes her head, smiling.

"I know I drive you crazy with all the planning and the thinking about planning, and the talking about thinking about planning a plan."

A half laugh, half sob bursts out of my mouth.

"It's okay," she laughs. "I drive myself crazy too. But it's just that—and maybe I should have talked to you about all this before—I can't really function without the planning. The whole thing—ACTION, BACKUP, CLEANUP, and always having a plan to deal with everything that could go wrong in your life? It's a coping strategy I've developed to help balance out some pretty severe anxiety."

I sit up straighter.

I never heard her use that word to describe herself before. I knew she was scared of heights, and that Dad's spontaneous side stressed her out sometimes. But I didn't realize she—like me—had a label for it.

"I've seen that same anxiety in you. Sometimes I even worry that I've made it worse, relying on you like I do to help with things maybe you're too young for." Mom sighs.

I fold my arms across my chest. Now even Mom is doubting me?

"I'm not too young," I say to the empty canyon. I sound like Janie insisting on peach pie.

"You're so responsible and amazing that it's easy to forget sometimes that you're a kid. Especially since you cope differently than I do," Mom says. "When you get anxious, you shut down, bottle things up inside. Like today. That's why I came up with the lemon drops all those years ago, to make talking about your feelings easier." Mom smiles into the camera.

Smiling at me.

"But sometimes it still takes me a minute to realize you're struggling. And I'm sorry." Her smile softens, sympathetic. "I hope you're ready to talk soon, so I can hear all the interesting thoughts in that unique Morgan brain of yours."

I bite my lip so hard I taste blood.

I wasted the last possible chance I had to talk to her, going to a disaster of a party instead.

"In the meantime, let me tell you a couple things about ABC planning that you might find comforting."

But instead of sagging in relief, my shoulders tense, rising up around my ears.

Comforting? I can't believe the universe just sent me a message from my mom the day she died, and it's about ABC planning.

Mom holds up a finger. "One. I didn't come up with this planning method to deliberately torture you, or to fix you. I share it with you because I believe it can help. Like it helped me. I learned—oh, boy did I learn—that we can't control what happens in our lives. All we can control is how ready we are. We *can* be ready for Plan B, should it arrive."

"No, we can't," I cry out. I'd fight with her about this right now if she were really here. I have Mom's broken promise as proof that sometimes—even with the best plans in the world— Plan B happens, and no amount of preparation and forethought will ever make us ready.

She holds up her second finger. "Two."

I swear she's really looking at me, and I don't blink or make a sound.

"Morgan Beth, you are the person who taught me the most important part of ABC planning. It's so important I'm sharing it with the world, instead of just with you."

Me? What could I have possibly taught her about my least favorite subject?

"You've always hated ABC planning." Mom laughs, remembering. "Even as a tiny girl, when I asked you to think of a Plan B, you'd squinch your face up, stomp your feet, and yell. Over time, I learned something crucial—you're not alone, Morgan. No one likes Plan B."

"Duh," I blurt. "So why are you still talking about it?"

"We spend our lives chasing Plan A," Mom says. "Because you were right. Plan B—"

Thunder rolls through the canyon, jolting my attention away from Mom. I'm suddenly aware of the chill in the air, spreading goose bumps over my arms.

I pause the video, because as badly as I want to hear the rest, gray clouds now cover the sun completely, leaving me and the rushing creek in ominous shadow.

Mountains of looming clouds.

Not cirrus.

Not cumulus.

Cumulonimbus.

As the next rumble thunders down the canyon, I launch to my feet. Pain shoots up my leg. I shouldn't walk on it, but I don't have a choice.

Those cumulonimbus clouds that don't lie are full to bursting with rain—rain that will have to go somewhere, even if it's through a slot canyon with narrowing walls hundreds of feet high and a limping twelve-year-old girl alone inside.

That's when I realize there really is something worse than Plan B forever.

Chapter 47

AFTER

I hardly recognize the third waterfall when I reach it.

Instead of the sparkling sandstone pool where we always stop and play, a murky rapid roars around the boulder we use as a slide, then rushes over the cliff's edge.

Even on a calm day, holding Dad's hand for support, I'm always nervous walking over the mouth of the waterfall to the footholds where we climb down.

Today the wider falls cover the footholds. Even my mountain goat of a dad would be swept away the second he tried to cross.

I drag myself out of the taunting, dragging current and perch precariously on a thin strip of sandstone bank under the overhanging canyon wall. Then I wrap my arms around myself to keep from freezing.

Once I'm over the falls, it's less than a mile to the visitor center. And I'll be safer, since the canyon below opens wide, spreading the water out. But up here, with narrow canyon walls closing in around me, if a flood comes . . . I squeeze my eyes closed, head spinning like I'm already in that breathless, unstoppable water.

Another peal of echoing thunder grumbles through the looming clouds, full to bursting with unshed rain.

Budge's hopeful voice rings in my head.

Play the game, Morgan. You'll find the solution.

"It's not a game, Bud." My voice breaks. "It's real life."

If the last few months have shown me anything, it's that real life doesn't always have a solution.

"Mom?" I call through chattering teeth.

No reply but the roaring, incessant water.

"Mom!" My yell drowns in the rushing waterfall. "Can I have a lemon drop? All the lemon drops?"

I have Janie's baggie, but I need more. Enough lemon drops to fill the stream and gush over the drop-off, making a waterfall of their own—Lemon Drop Falls.

"Please! I'm ready, now. Come back."

No answer—not even the hint of her presence. Just the tangible feeling of rain—so moist and thick it's like I'm wrapped up in one of those cumulonimbus clouds.

Why did I send her away? I need her with me now more than I have ever needed anything.

With fumbling, prune-shriveled fingers, I pull out my phone.

And there she is.

I nearly sob with relief.

It's only miniature Mom, in her bright purple tee shirt, jeans, and ponytail. But like Janie and Budge singing "Edelweiss" on the trail to Cassidy Arch, it's enough to help me catch a breath.

I turn the volume to max so I can hear her over the rushing waterfall.

"You were right all along, Morgan. Plan B sucks."

I nod, tears spilling over.

"I mean, sometimes Plan B is cereal and bananas instead of toast and jam when your little brother ate all the bread," Mom laughs. "The answer then is get over it and eat your puffed oat squares, you know? But other times? When Plan B is all that's left after life's greatest disappointments?" Her voice goes quiet, and I pull the phone closer. "Plan B can be almost impossible to accept. Believe me. I know." Her mouth twists, eyes shining with tears.

She *knows*?

What Plan A did she lose? Was *she* living in Plan B too?

The thought raises the hair on the back of my neck.

"But if Plan B is so bad," she asks, "how can we ever be happy again?"

"Right." I rub trembling hands over my arms to warm them.

"That's the thing, Morgan." Mom pauses, her voice breaking. "Plan B isn't going to make you happy again. It can't."

My whole body slumps. I know I shouldn't be disappointed. It's the truth, and I knew it before she did. But she looked like she had an answer. Like her words on this video could show me a way back to being best friends with Keilani and Hrishi. A way over a waterfall where I'm stranded alone.

A way back to the life we lost when she died.

And of course—of *course*—there can't be a way back.

But she's smiling through her tears. And not just any smile.

It's how she looked on my eleventh birthday when she was about to burst from not telling me that my birthday card held season tickets to Royals women's soccer.

I strain to hear her next words.

"Plan B," Mom says slowly and clearly like these are the most important words ever spoken, "was never intended to be a place to stay."

She beams like she just revealed the meaning of the universe.

I shake my head.

How is that supposed to comfort me when I'm stuck in Plan B forever?

"Plan B is a place of transition and transformation," Mom says. "A safe place to rest while we're hurting."

"Not that safe," I whisper.

"It's a place for reaching out to people who love us, so they can help find solutions," she says. "I hate to break it to you, Morgan, but I'll probably keep reminding you about Plan B forever, because I know how special it can be. It's more than just a soft landing when you fall from Plan A. Plan B is the launching pad you use to propel yourself to something brand new. To a New Plan A. And your New Plan A will hold possibilities you may never have imagined."

Mom leans forward like she's trying to come through the camera and grab me by the shoulders. "Plan B only exists to help us reach a new Plan A."

I pause the video and lurch unsteadily to my feet. The move sends a stab of pain through my ankle, but I don't care.

A new Plan A?

I don't know what to do with her words, and the strange, terrible hope they spark in me. Could a new Plan A—one where I could actually be happy—exist?

Suddenly, my phone starts having some sort of fit, buzzing and dinging so wildly I nearly drop it. Notifications pop up over Mom's video—texts.

Impossibly, I've got reception.

And texts from Keilani.

> Missed you at soccer.

> Maybe call me sometime.

From Dad too.

> Morgan, where are you?

> Please respond if you get coverage.

> Whatever is wrong, we can work it out.

> I'm so worried, Morgan. Please!

The last text sends chills down my spine.

> IF YOU FIND THIS PHONE PLEASE CALL
> 555-424-8445. MY DAUGHTER IS MISSING

Wait. If I can receive texts, I can send them, tell Dad where I am, and get help.

I frantically press reply.

```
I'm at the third waterfall
```

My fingers are pruney, cold-stiff, and swollen, and it's hard to make them text at all.

```
I can't get over
```

```
can you come?
```

I hold the phone in my shaking hand, watching my messages. Each reads: *trying to send.*

"Try harder."

I step into the rushing current and fight toward the boulder in the middle of the pool. I scrape my shins, scrambling to the top, and stand with my weight on my left foot. I've got to get the phone higher, closer to the phone signal.

Trying to send.

Come on.

My good leg cramps, so I shift my weight, but my right ankle collapses, tipping me forward. In slow motion, I fumble the phone with sausage fingers.

It falls end over end, splashing into the surging creek.

I slide down the mud-covered boulder, lunging after my only tangible connection with my family—Mom's pictures, my careful plans for the trip and beyond, any chance to get Dad to save me, and Mom herself, here with me when I need her most and maybe about to tell me how to escape Plan B forever.

My grasping fingers brush against the phone case as it washes over the edge of the waterfall.

"Mom!" I yell, like it's really her falling into the vast stone basin at the bottom of the falls, vanishing beneath the surging water.

The creek batters me against the stone side of the pool, wanting to carry me over and down like Mom's phone. But I drag myself onto the sandstone ledge where we usually wait for Dad to help us cross the mouth of the waterfall.

I'm not sure if the clouds are thicker than before, or if the dark means the sun is setting. Either way, soon there will be no light for searchers to find me, even if they knew where to look.

No plan—A, B, or C—can fix this.

So I don't try to plan. Instead, I curl up on the last Morgan-sized spot of ground between a raging creek and an uncrossable waterfall. I press my face against my fish-cold knees, holding myself so tight.

And finally, I let the tears flow, sobbing out everything left inside me while I listen to the troubled water beside me fall and fall and fall.

Chapter 48

AFTER

(By one month)

Until May third, I had two best friends.

That's the day I messed things up with Hrishi, but it wasn't until Brownie Night, a couple of weeks later, that I lost Keilani too.

Maybe if I hadn't just heard Dad on another call with Grandma Bell talking about applying for new jobs, things would have turned out differently.

And maybe if Keilani hadn't brought Mackelle with her.

Or if she'd brought cookies instead of Mom's famous brownie recipe.

Or maybe if I'd had any part of me that wasn't all the way broken.

In that other version of Brownie Night, we might have ended up talking, laughing, and crying—flat on our backs on the trampoline. Watching the stars, like that one night in Capitol Reef.

Only this time, Keilani would have comforted me instead of the other way around. And I'd have been the one reminding her that we'd be best friends forever.

But she did bring Mackelle. And Mom's brownies. And

I wasn't Before-Morgan anymore. I was After-Morgan. Plan-B-Morgan.

Dad was still on the phone with Grandma when Keilani and Mackelle showed up on our front porch.

"We made these to cheer you up." Mackelle's face scrunched with pity. "We're so sorry for your loss."

I didn't know which made me more angry—"*We* made these" or "*We're* so sorry for your loss."

"And also," Mackelle said quickly. "They're kind of to apologize. For what happened at the pool party, and with Hrishi and the painting. It got pretty out of hand, and I was trying—"

My glare cut her off. As it turned out, what made me maddest was her totally fake apology.

"They're Mama Bell's brownies," Keilani said softly, like I needed the clarification. Her eyes were shiny.

I blinked quickly. I didn't need "we" seeing my eyes get shiny too.

Keilani held out the white paper plate, but instead of taking them, I folded my arms across my chest.

"It's just . . ." Keilani cleared her throat. "I know it must be really hard. I've been missing her so much."

Her eyes did more than shine now. Big tears threatened to spill over. Mackelle put a comforting hand on her shoulder.

Angry heat spread over my face.

Why hadn't Keilani come over here to make Mom's brownies with me?

Why was she the one crying right now?

Why did she need Mackelle, with her super-fake sympathy face, to comfort her?

"I know it's not the same," Keilani said. "But I know what it's like to live without my mom too."

Mackelle nodded like she also knew what it was like.

I balled my hands into fists at my sides.

"And your mom was like a second mom for me. Losing her has been so ha—"

"You're right!" My tone was sharp, and Keilani flinched. "It's not the same. You have no idea what it's like."

"I . . . I know. It's just—"

"My mom is dead!" I yelled. "Is your mom dead?"

Keilani gasped, her mouth dropping open. Fishy Mackelle mirrored her expression.

I knew I should stop, but I was too full of shaking rage that I didn't know I had in me until right that minute.

"No," I answered for her. "Your mom is alive, but you *chose* to live without her. Like you didn't even care about her. So don't tell me you know what I'm feeling, and she was your second mom, and it's been so hard for *you*."

Keilani made a sound like my words had cut her. It made my own tears spill over, and I swiped angrily at my face with the back of my hand.

"Why don't you and your new best friend take my dead mom's brownies and leave me alone!"

"Morgan!" Keilani's voice was a sob.

"Come on." Mackelle pulled her back. "Let's go."

For one terrible moment, I watched Keilani hesitate. Even after the hateful words I'd hurled at her, part of me hoped she'd send Mackelle away and throw her arms around me and refuse to leave me.

Best friends forever.

But Mackelle said, "Come on," again. And that was all it took.

I could hear Keilani crying, asking what she'd done wrong, as Mackelle led her away.

I crumpled up on my porch, sobbing like my heart would break.

It was the first time I'd cried since Hrishi walked away and left my shoes unkicked at Mom's funeral.

Chapter 49

AFTER

I'm not sure how long I huddle, crying under the moist, heavy sky, next to the relentless waterfall. Long enough that after I stop, I still do those little-kid hiccup-sobs every few seconds.

If Dad *were* here, he'd say . . . Actually, for once, I have no idea what he'd say. Or Budge, or Janie. This situation is pretty much unprecedented.

Mom, however, is too predictable. She'd say this is as good a time as any for a strong Plan B.

The waterfall doesn't look any more passable than before. The cloudy sky still looms over me, full to bursting with its own unshed tears. And I still can't imagine crossing the gushing waterfall without Dad.

But I smile, in spite of everything.

Mom agreed that Plan B is awful. What was it she said?

Suddenly, missing phone or no, I remember her voice, her mannerisms, like she's here talking. I don't need a video—her words are inside me.

Plan B was never intended to be a place to stay.

Plan B is the launching pad you use to propel yourself to

something brand new. To a New Plan A. And your New Plan A will hold possibilities you may never have imagined.

Plan B only exists to help us reach a new Plan A.

A tiny flutter stirs in my chest—hope, I think.

Suddenly even though I'm still trapped high up in a narrow canyon at an impassable waterfall, with a possible flood on the way, things don't feel quite as terrible as they did a minute before.

If I make it back, is it possible that we don't have to keep living in Plan B?

I stir, my cramped muscles fighting like old chewing gum that's lost all its give.

Come on, Morgan, Dad says. *We always finish the hike. One foot in front of the other.*

I place my open palms on the rock behind me, steadying myself as my eyes follow the water. It plunges into the wider-and-deeper-than-ever pool below. Then it reaches the tumbling creek bed, following the canyon down and out.

Endlessly moving on to somewhere it's never seen before.

Our best adventure yet, imaginary Janie sighs.

That tiny, growing hope pulls me to a stand. The calmer waters of the widening creek flow on below the falls, barely beyond my reach.

I'm not going to stay here anymore.

Yes! Budge-in-my-head says. *Every game has a solution. Look at it another way.*

A surprised laugh bursts out of my mouth.

"Mom! I know where he got that line. You were self-helping

him through video games, weren't you? When he'd freak out over losing a million times? Every game has a solution if you look at it another way? That's ABC planning. And Janie with her every-challenge-is-an-adventure attitude? That's you too."

What if I do what Mom-via-Budge-and-Janie-in-my-head suggested? What if I see this as an adventure, and look at it another way?

For maybe the first time, I don't mind Mom's self-help. I obviously can't figure this out on my own.

Not on your own. Best friends forever, whispers Keilani, who still wants me to "maybe call her sometime" even after those awful things I said.

Am I brave enough?

For the Republic! cheers Hrishi-in-my-mind. *I dare you!*

I look once more at the waterfall plunging to the base of the falls. But this time I see it from the water's point of view—no hesitation as it leaps without fear into the wider, deeper pool below, then follows its own path out.

Wider and deeper might mean I haven't got my same path over the falls, but also, maybe it's opened a new way.

"Okay, guys," I whisper. "I think I'm ready."

This tiny patch of dry rock is my launching pad, and I'm going somewhere new.

I take a deep breath, plug my nose, and . . . jump.

Chapter 50

NOW

I leap over the mouth of Lemon Drop Falls, my stomach in my throat as I plummet. The cold water slaps me as I plunge into the roiling pool.

I never touch the sandy bottom—that's how deeper-than-ever the water is. I swim desperately to the surface, gasping and choking as I flail through the murky water. Then I stagger onto dryish land like a mud-red sea creature with flood grass clinging to my legs.

Wiping the water from my eyes, I look back up at the tiny spot of rock where I huddled hopelessly a minute before.

"I did it!" I yell.

The voices of my family and friends in my mind gave me the ideas, the courage.

"We did it!" My words echo off the canyon walls, bouncing around me triumphantly.

It's still a bit of a slog to the visitor center, but with the wider canyon opening up dry ground on the creek banks, I soon find a solid stick I can use to help me hobble along. With every halting step, I wonder: What would a new Plan A look like? What would I want it to look like?

Can I talk to Dad about these questions? Let him help me figure it out?

All the words I've been needing to say and holding back rise up in my throat, and I hold my breath, wondering if I'm brave enough—and possibly, if this could be what "being brave for them" looks like.

As I limp around the bend in the canyon, tentative rays of sun—now hanging low in the eastern sky—break through the clouds.

I'm going to do it. I'm going to have five thousand lemon drops if that's what it takes to help me get through everything I need to say.

"Dad!" I shout. "I'm here!"

My voice echoes back—those two words, "I'm here." They come over and over, until I realize it's not two words, but one.

"Morgan!"

It's not until I see Dad with one short ranger and the giant one with the curly hair coming around the bend in the creek toward me that I'm sure I'm not imagining his voice.

His entire body is sharp edges, head turning from side to side as he searches for me.

"Dad!" I drop my stick and limp toward him as fast as my ankle will let me, waving both arms frantically.

I know the exact moment he sees me, because he stops in his tracks, then breaks into a run like this is a racetrack instead of a rocky stream bed.

"Morgan!"

Then I'm laughing and crying with his arms around me, his old camp tee shirt rough against my face. He smells like campfire and sweat and safety, and he says my name over and over, holding me so tight I can hardly breathe.

"How did you find me? Did Budge give you the note I wrote on the trail map?"

"There wasn't a note. Budgie only had a—oh. A paper airplane he made out of a map." Dad slaps his forehead, and a giggle escapes my lips.

"That boy." He shakes his head. "No. Your texts came through at the ranger's station, and I basically sprinted straight here. Thank God you're okay." He holds me at arm's length. "You *are* okay, aren't you?"

I can't say the words I always say.

I'm not okay.

I think I will be, but only if I stop holding everything inside.

Yes. Open your mouth and tell him what you need . . . what you want. It's not exactly Almost-Mom in my head this time. It's more just me, thinking what she would say. Maybe it always was.

"Dad—"

"Dude!" says a familiar voice. "You found her."

The big ranger with the curly hair splashes up to us, while his short-legged partner barks into his walkie-talkie, "Subject found in Sulphur Creek!"

"Girl, you okay?" Ranger Dude asks.

"I'm not hurt," I say. It's only a little lie. My ankle might be sprained, but it will heal, and I need the ranger to go so I can talk to Dad before my courage fades.

Ranger Dude shakes his curly head. "You know you broke the first rule of hiking safety—always hike with a partner. This dude was freaking out." He slaps Dad on the back with his large, meaty hand. "You guys need help getting back?"

"We're good. Thank you," Dad says. "We'll hurry back for my other kids."

"No worries. Your kids are chillin' with Ranger Sarah, identifying every rock sample in the visitor center. Take a minute if you need it."

"Thank you," Dad says. "Could you let them know we've found her, and we'll be there soon?"

Big, curly ranger nods, and his partner speaks into his walkie-talkie again as they both head up the hill toward the visitor center. "No medical assistance needed. Subject is fine. I repeat, subject is fine."

Again, my brain glitches on the inaccurate sentence.

"Dad—"

"Oh, Morgan. You're safe. You're here . . . and—" His tone changes from relief to distress in an instant. "I can't believe you. I can't . . . Why? Why would you ever do something this . . . this—" He drags his hand through his messy hair instead of speaking—all out of words to describe this thing I've done. "What were you thinking?"

Two and a half months of trying to avoid telling him just that rise up in my throat, choking me.

You can do this. Almost-Mom's whisper helps me open my mouth.

"Dad—" I shift on my feet, wincing as my weight falls on my injured ankle.

"You *are* hurt!" Dad grabs my arm. "Sit down and let me see." He half carries me to a flat rock beside the creek.

"Dad—"

"Let's get your sandal off. Hey!" he calls after the now-distant rangers.

"No, Dad!" I put a hand on his shoulder. "I twisted my ankle hours ago. It hurts." My voice gets louder with every sentence. "But it's not broken and I don't need the rangers. I need—"

Why didn't I use the whole walk down the canyon to figure out what to say first? I need everything. *Everything.* My friends, soccer, time to myself, school supplies, clothes that fit?

Say something. Anything.

"I need a bra!" My face goes hot. I can't believe that's the first thing to burst out of my mouth.

"What?" Dad says.

"A bra." I'm not about to stop now. "I need a bra super bad."

"You're not wearing a bra?" he chokes out.

"Holy cow. Of course I'm wearing a bra. I mean like a new bra—or two or three. And not like the training bras Mom bought me last fall, because I am totally going to have to change in front of other people in PE next year, and I can't be wearing this piece of cloth pretending to be a bra. And Mom was going to buy me one but we didn't, and that's on me because I was so, so stupid."

"Whoa, what? Hold on."

If I wait, I'm afraid I'll stop.

"Also, my shoes don't fit, and none of my jeans do either. In our Human Growth and Development talk, the school nurse said puberty makes your hips bigger, and mine are. Which means I need new underwear too. Besides, I'm twelve years old, and I cannot keep wearing Hello Kitty. Mackelle would die laughing, and I'd probably punch her and get suspended or arrested or something."

Dad's jaw drops.

Shock I can deal with. I don't want him to be hurt, but so far, he just looks windblown, like he's been tossed about by a Morgan-shaped cyclone.

"And pads," I blurt. "Like, for my period. You should get them now because it'll be bad if I don't have them when I start, and—"

A short laugh bursts out of him, cutting me off.

"What?" I fold my arms, defensive.

"I'm sorry." He wipes his expression clean of any trace of laughter. "I promise I'm not laughing at you, it's just . . . I've been freaking out for hours, and you're safe, and I'm pretty sure you were still a kid when I last saw you this morning. And now *this* is the topic of conversation?" He runs a hand over his face and into his messy hair.

"This has to be the topic of conversation." I look right into his eyes. "All of this. It can't wait."

"You're right." His voice is serious. "Talking like this has waited way too long."

I pull out the bag of lemon drops, open the seal. I pass them to Dad, and his eyes widen.

"We might need these," I say. "Like, all of them."

Chapter 51

"**W**ow," Dad says, when I finally pause for breath. "Just . . . wow." He's got that windblown look again— like he barely survived a Morgan-shaped tornado.

I've been going Janie-speed for at least twenty minutes, talking about everything from babysitting to soccer, school supplies to friend drama, and even boy troubles.

"Sorry," I say, suddenly sheepish. "It's just—"

"Don't apologize." He's watching me with so much Fog-free focus I almost can't meet his gaze. "Never, ever apologize for talking to me, okay?"

I nod.

"Like, apologize for leaving the milk out. Apologize for painting graffiti on the school . . ."

I wince. After Mom died, Dad still had to pay for the damages, and when I told him I needed to earn the money myself, he said I'd more than earned it helping with Budge and Janie. But he still had to write the check, and I still feel bad about it.

"Maybe apologize for running away, initiating Search and Rescue protocols, and scaring me half out of my mind. But don't ever apologize for talking to me. From you, I want to hear *all the words*. Got it?"

"Got it," The start of a smile tugs up the corner of my mouth, and Dad pulls me into a fierce hug.

"Good." He pulls away to look at me with serious eyes. "Because all that stuff you said? There's a lot I don't understand yet. A lot we still need to talk about."

"Yeah."

He's right. Three months of no talking won't fit into fifteen frantic minutes. I look back at the creek, glistening golden as the sun dips toward the horizon, and as the weight of that vast lot of un-talked-about things settles over both of us.

"I know you usually talked to your mom. And I know I'm a lousy substitute."

"No, Dad. You're not . . ." But I don't know what to say. It's true that no one can replace Mom. "Some of this stuff is just hard to explain." A tear slips down my cheek.

"Try." He wipes away my tear with his thumb. "I'm here, Morgan. And I love you. Help me understand. Maybe start with soccer. I didn't get that part. Why wouldn't you play soccer this fall?"

I stare down at my bedraggled, sand-crusted sandals. "It doesn't seem like an option anymore, now that Mom—"

He shakes his head, bewildered. "Of course it's an option. I know we've all had to sacrifice some things with your mom gone, but not something this important to you. Besides, how would your team survive without their starting right forward?"

He holds out his fist for a bump, but my hands, clenched tight together in my lap, leave him hanging.

"They *have* a starting right forward." The words taste wrong in my mouth, and I spit them out. "It's Mackelle, and she'll do so great they won't even miss me. But that's not the whole problem."

"Okay. Tell me the rest." He says he wants to know, but his shoulders rise along with his stress—just what I was trying to avoid.

My words come out small. "Who's going to drive carpool, and calendar the games, and watch Budge and Janie while I'm at practice five days a week? You're so busy with work and all your deadlines."

"We'll figure it out," he says.

"And how will we pay for club fees without Mom's income?"

His eyes widen. But he asked for the rest, so I'm telling him, even though it feels like I'm giving him a drink from a fire hose.

"I'll take care of it," Dad says.

"I can't play soccer anyway." I look away. "Tryouts were in June, and I didn't go. So I'm not even on the team."

"Wait, what?"

I bite down on my lip.

"Did you know when tryouts were?"

"Yeah, but things were so—"

"And you didn't feel like you could tell me. And I didn't think to ask."

I press my lips together, watching as understanding dawns on him.

Dad shakes his head. "I didn't plan for the fall season. Didn't know what needed to be done."

He blinks, like he's seeing a whole new world, and he hates the look of it.

"It wasn't your fault," I whisper. "I know you were trying. It was just . . . The Fog."

He looks at me for a long moment, and then nods slowly, without asking what I mean. Then he slips a gentle arm around me, and we both stare down at the creek, shining so bright now it burns my eyes.

"It's just . . . without your mom . . ." The words sigh out of him, blowing away on the breeze.

"Yeah."

"She juggled a million things—gracefully. And since she died . . ." He flails his baffled hands in the air. "It's just . . . balls. Balls everywhere." Dad's voice breaks and his face twitches like he's not sure whether to laugh or cry.

He clears his throat. "I dropped the ball, Morgan. And you picked it up. And I've been letting you. I told myself the way we managed this summer was okay for now, since we were in survival mode." His lips wobble.

"It's okay." I put a hand on his arm.

He shakes his head. "It's not. You're a kid, Morgan. And I'm your parent. And I'm sorry." His eyes shine with unshed tears. "I've let you down. And somehow, I didn't even realize it. The Fog? Was that what you called it?"

Suddenly the tangle in my mind unravels a bit more.

"It wasn't just The Fog." I know the words are true as I say them, and I force myself to speak clearly, even though I still wish I could hide. Maybe when Mom told me to be brave, she meant this. I'm not sure, but the words feel brave when I say them.

"I didn't want you to see . . . the balls."

Dad makes a weird half-laugh, half-sob sound in his throat.

"I picked them up and hid them on purpose," I say quickly, "because I didn't want you to see them and be sad."

"Oh, Morgan—" He grabs hold of my hand, and my tears spill over.

"I didn't want all of us to be sad. Didn't want you to worry about me. Didn't want you to move us away from our friends and our home to Grandma Bell in Michigan because it's too hard for you to do things without Mom."

He gasps, but I can't stop now. Not when I finally have the words and the courage at the same time.

"I had to pretend things were okay to give me enough time to fix things."

"No, Morgan." Dad puts a hand on my shoulder, and when I look up, his face is crumpled, slick with tears. "There's nothing you had to do."

"But I promised Mom. I *promised* her . . ." I squeeze my eyes tight shut, tears flowing down my face.

"Promised her what?"

"The night she died . . . Mom told me to be brave for you guys. To keep you safe. To help you be happy."

"Oh, Morgan—"

"And I tried. I'm still . . . trying—" My voice breaks. "So hard."

"Of course you are."

"And I know we might have to move, still." My shoulders shake with a sob. "I'm not a little kid anymore, and I can be brave about that. I can do it if we need to."

"Of course you can." Dad pulls me into his arms then, and that undoes my last bit of resistance.

"I miss her," I sob against his shoulder. "I try not to, but I miss her so bad, Dad. I still . . . need her."

"Of course you do, sweetheart." He holds on to me so tight, while my hot tears soak into the rough fabric of his old tee shirt. "So do I." His shoulders shake as he cries.

I don't pull away. I don't say I'm fine. I don't try to fix anything. I just hold on to my dad. We hold on to each other while the flood of emotion pours through us, and neither of us tries to stop it.

Chapter 52

A MISSING PIECE OF MEMORY

Mom's hand on my hair, leaving the spaghetti for something more important. Always ready for a lemon drop. Always. Her shallow breaths, sighing in and out under my cheek. Her arms around me, holding me together.

"Oh, Mom. I messed everything up so bad. With Hrishi and Keilani and Mackelle. With you."

"Not with me, Morgan Beth. Never with me. And it'll be all right. There's nothing you can't fix."

"*You* can say that. *You* always fix everything. Like it's easy for you."

A barely there laugh, shaking her chest.

"I don't know how I've given you that impression. But it's almost never true. I don't always fix things, and when I do, it's far from easy."

"But you said making things better was in your job description. I think making things worse is in mine."

"Oh, sweetheart."

More crying. More holding.

"No one has that kind of power . . . to make everything better. Most of us just have to put one foot in front of the other—like

Dad always says about hiking. It works on mountains, and I've found it often works in life too."

Chapter 53

NOW

After the flood of crying ebbs away, Dad and I hold on to each other, breathing in and out until I notice a familiar feeling—that unbuttoned feeling, open and safe—like after the rain dancing.

When he finally pulls away, it's a little easier to look up at him, now that I'm not holding in any more earth-shattering secrets.

Dad takes a deep breath. "All right, Morgan. I've got two things I need to say. Number One: your mom might have needed you to watch over the kids while the paramedics were wheeling her away, but she was *not* telling you it was your permanent job to keep everyone safe and happy forever. Okay?"

The Morgan of the last few months wants to protest, but his words feel solid, steady.

True.

"Okay."

"Number Two: is it my fault that you're hurting, Morgan?"

I shake my head.

"Right. And when I'm hurting . . . when we all do . . ." He

looks right into my eyes, all serious, without a wisp of Fog. "I need you to understand it's not your fault either."

His words click into place in my mind, and a sigh slips out of me, as more tension I didn't even know I was holding drifts away on the canyon breeze.

"Okay."

He holds up three fingers. "Number Three."

I give him a skeptical look. "You said two things."

"Well, I'm no Mom," he says. "And clearly, I'm terrible at lists. I'm just making this up as I go along. Which is the point of Number Three. I'm as new to this life-without-Mom thing as you are, and I'm trying, but I'm probably going to keep missing things. Which means you've got to talk to me. I need you to stop protecting my feelings and trust me to handle it. Deal?"

"Deal." I bite my lip, sheepish.

"And Number Four—"

"Four?" A little laugh escapes me.

He waves my objection away. "Whoever heard of a three-item list? Number Four is you've got to trust me not to do something crazy that will break your world apart without even consulting you."

I cock my head at him, confused.

"We are not moving to Michigan to live with Grandma."

"Wait, we're not? Like definitely not?" I feel a full smile break over my face for the first time in . . . months, maybe.

"No. Where did you get that idea?"

"I heard you. On the phone. And . . ." The memory lingers,

heavy all around me, but I refuse to let it button me back up. "You said money was tight too."

Dad puts his palm to his forehead. "The week I went back to work, when I called Grandma. You heard that?"

"Yeah. And last week too. Talking about job applications."

"Wow." He grabs my earlobe, tugs on it, pretends to look inside my ear. "That's some impressive hearing you've developed."

"But *are* you?" I can't be derailed by his teasing. "Getting a new job?"

He nods slowly. "I can see now that I should have told you before. But I didn't want to get your hopes up before it was settled. Too much of our life has been so uncertain, lately."

I inhale quickly, feel my shoulders rise. Uncertain is an understatement. Everyday life has felt like Hrishi double bouncing me while I try to think of answers to awkward Truth or Dare questions.

"But we're in final salary negotiations. And the job's local," Dad says quickly. "Pays a little more too. But the main point is I'll be able to do most of my work from home."

"From home?" I lift my gaze to meet his.

He's smiling, and his eyebrows do a quick double-rise.

"I'll still be working a lot. And sometimes for long hours. But I'll be able to take breaks to help you get started on homework after school, fix dinner most nights. And drive you to soccer."

"But—"

"And I'm getting that coach on the phone first thing when we get home," he says. "They'd be nuts not to take you back."

I take in a deep breath, as my brain lights up with ideas. Me, over at Hrishi's for dinner without worrying about Budge and Janie. Soccer practice with Blue Thunder. Making new friends at junior high and possibly inviting them over.

Wow. This feels like the start of . . . a New Plan A.

I put a hand over my chest, where I can feel the button, trying to close me up again.

"What is it?" Dad asks. "Tell me what's wrong."

I want to. But the whole idea is slippery in my mind.

"It's just . . . I think another reason I never talked to you is it felt wrong to . . . still *feels* wrong to want things. Like it's not fair to Mom."

"Like we don't love her enough if we don't stay miserable forever?" Dad nods slowly like he's felt it too. "Why do you think we're camping in August and not in June like usual? It took me this long to decide it's okay to go without her."

"I sort of thought we were stuck in Plan B forever," I say. "Since Plan A was that Mom would . . . still be here."

"I know." He nods, solemnly. "But Plan B sucks."

I laugh. Partly because that word is not allowed in our house, and partly because it's nice to know both my parents agree with me on this.

"Yeah," I say. "But on the hike today I found this video Mom made for her channel, a message she recorded specially for me, and—Oh, no. Dad!"

"What?" He straightens up, his voice sharp with worry.

"The video's gone." My eyes burn with tears, and I blink

fast, not ready to start crying all over again. "I was watching it and then I texted you and it washed away in the creek and now it's gone, and Mom's phone too. I know it's so expensive, and I promise to earn money to—"

"It's a thing, Morgan. Don't worry. We'll figure it out."

"The video's not a thing." I see the phone holding Mom's final words to me tumbling end over end into the surging, murky water.

"Hold on. You know your mother. When did she ever *not* have a Plan B? If there's one thing I know, it's that Eve had *everything* double backed-up in the cloud. I promise you that video is waiting for you safe and sound, where you can watch it over and over forever."

"Ohhh." The loss and fear drain out of me and I sag against him. "The thing is . . . from what she said in her message, I think Mom would want us to have a New Plan A."

He gives my shoulder a squeeze. "A hundred percent agree."

"Really?"

"Yeah. If we do, maybe she'll stop haunting my dreams demanding it."

I lean my head against Dad's shoulder, but I'm barely settled when I remember something important and pull away to look at him.

"I have a question."

"Anything."

"In the video Mom said she knew what it felt like to lose Plan A, and she looked so sad. What Plan A did she lose?"

Dad's silence stretches out long enough to make me nervous. "You said anything."

"For sure." He nods quickly. "It's just . . . Mom and I made the choice—maybe the wrong choice—not to tell you kids." He blows out a quick breath. "You know how there's such a big gap between you and Janie? Well, Mom's body had trouble carrying babies. During that time, she lost a few pregnancies before they had a chance to grow. And before you . . . there was one that . . . Well." Dad runs a hand through his hair. "Morgan, you were not our first child."

The world seems to tip off balance. "What?"

"We had a son first—stillborn at twenty-two weeks."

I scan his face. "Wait, I had an older brother?"

Dad nods, a faraway look in his eyes. "We called him Zachary. He was so small—small enough he fit in my hand."

I can hardly imagine a person that small. A person who could have lived. Could have grown up and—suddenly my mind is full of images of a blond-haired, soccer-playing, laughing boy, a little older than me.

"But . . . I would have wanted to . . . I do want to know about him. Do you have pictures?"

Dad shakes his head. "Just his hand and footprints in plaster, the tiny white blanket we wrapped him in—tucked away in Mom's treasure box."

"A big brother! What if he had lived? How old would he be? Wait! I wouldn't even be the oldest." I pause, mind blown, as reality rearranges itself in my head. "We could have played soccer together, built forts. We could have been best friends maybe."

But Dad shakes his head.

"Mom got pregnant with you two months after Zachary was born so early. We hadn't planned to try again so soon, but you were a surprise, a miracle. You showed up right when you should have."

"But still, if—" Then it dawns on me. "If Zachary had been born when he should've . . . if he had lived . . . Mom wouldn't have gotten pregnant with me. I wouldn't even be here."

Dad nods.

"So wait, I was . . . *I* was Plan B?" I feel the solid ground slipping away beneath me.

Dad shakes his head, cupping my face with both hands. "Not Plan B. What did Mom's message say? Think, Morgan."

I do. And it doesn't take long. Mom's secret smile that promised hope after pain.

"Not Plan B," I whisper. "I was her New Plan A."

He nods.

Images of Mom fill my mind—tucking me in at night, cheering wild and free at my soccer games, throwing her arms around me. Telling me she was "team Morgan for life."

Loving me—her New Plan A.

My eyes fill with tears again, but not sad this time. More like too much sunlight in my eyes.

"Mom loved her New Plan A." That knowledge flows through

me like the clear water of the creek below. Makes me feel open, steady. Ready for something brand new.

Dad nods again. "We both did. Loving your New Plan A doesn't mean you loved the original Plan A any less. And emerging from that pain and loss with a New Plan A made your mom who she was. It helped her guide a lot of people so they could be happy again too."

"Like she guided me today."

"And me most days."

"She's still with us, isn't she?"

Dad laughs. "I can't look around a corner without hearing her voice in my head. What she'd say, what she'd do. What she'd plan for us if she were here."

I give him a sharp look. "You hear her too?"

Dad's face is golden with the light of the sun hanging low on the horizon. "Not like an actual voice, you know. But sometimes she's pretty real in my head."

I nod, and we share a look of perfect understanding.

"Mom and I built this family together," Dad says. "She'll always be in the places we go. In the traditions we keep. In the plans we make."

I remember the echoes of Mom in the voice of every family member on top of the third waterfall.

"In us," I whisper.

We watch in silence as the sun, barely peeking through the clouds, dips below the western horizon. Sunset glow spreads across sky and land, turning everything it touches to magic.

The final view of the Sulphur Creek hike blazes like it's on fire, the silence shimmering with hope and anticipation.

The wind brushes my face, a gentle touch of hope. And I can feel Mom's approval, as warm and real as Dad's arm around my shoulders.

As the sunset glow begins to fade, Dad finally says, "All right. Let's go get—"

"Our New Plan A," I finish his sentence.

"Well, I was thinking we'd get your siblings—rescue the rangers from their junior assistants. But a New Plan A sounds good too."

I laugh and start to stand, but before I'm steady on my feet, Dad scoops me into his arms, carrying me toward the visitor center.

"I'm too big," I say.

"I'm super buff—like Thor, basically. I could carry you pretty much all day." His voice is a grunt, though, like my preteen body is killing him a little bit.

"Put me down," I laugh. "I can walk. Just let me lean on you."

He looks at me for a moment, then he nods once, lowering me gently to the ground. He puts his arm around me so I can use his strength for support.

"You realize we're not done talking," Dad says as we limp around together toward the visitor center. "You're like what, eleven?"

My jaw drops, indignant. "Twelve."

"Too young for *boy* trouble," he grumbles. "And since when does *Hrishi* count as a boy?"

"He didn't—he doesn't." My face flames, even in the cool, dusk breeze. "I think I'll fix things with Keilani first, and let her help me with Hrishi," I say. "Rather than talk to my dad about boys."

Dad gives me a wounded look. "I'll have you know I'm kind of an expert."

"Daaad."

"Like not to toot my own horn, but I actually *am* a boy."

I roll my eyes. "I'm adding Dad Not Teasing Me to every day of my new master plan."

"*Our* new master plan," he corrects me as we arrive at the door to the visitor center. "And I wouldn't add No Teasing to the plan just yet. Let's wait and see."

Knowing Dad, I'd imagine there will be plenty of wait-and-seeing in our New Plan A.

But also planning. Both are in my blood, after all.

We'll have to figure out the perfect balance together.

Chapter 54

THE NEW PLAN A

In the blazing September sun, Blue Thunder plays the Warriors for the first time since Soccer-pocalypse last spring—up two to one, near the end of the second half.

Sweat pours down my face as I shout and jump on the sidelines, cheering like a World Cup Final fan in the second period of overtime.

Keilani swipes the ball from two of their midfielders at once, dribbling it up the field like an extension of her body as she looks for a pass. But the Warriors' left defender is all *over* Mackelle, and Tasha hasn't caught up since the momentum of the game switched so fast.

"Go, go!" I scream. "All the way." Beside me, Hrishi waves his dilapidated favorite sign.

He yells even louder than me. "Yes! Score one for the Republic!"

Keilani only hesitates for a second, setting up her shot. She swings back, then makes contact with the ball. It flies true over the head of the Warriors' super-keeper, swishing back against the net.

And the crowd goes wild.

Keilani's dad is yelling something in his deep voice with one fist in the air. But it's me and Hrishi that go berserk. High-fiving and hugging, and mangling his poster.

It feels perfect to be here with him, cheering for Keilani. She deserved that goal. She owned it!

"Morgan!" Coach shouts. "Get over here! Now! You're in for Tasha on left forward." She glares at me for losing my mind when I should have been stretching.

I sprint to the line. "Sorry, Coach." I wait the half second for the ref's whistle, then fly into the game.

"Just finish it," Coach yells after me. That's what she calls me, Keilani, and Mackelle—her finishers.

We've been drilling together ever since the doctor said I could train on my ankle again. It's paid off too. By now, we don't even have to guess what each other is thinking. And I'm getting really comfortable with my new position as starting left forward.

Full of fresh energy from subbing out, I roar into the game—in and out of open spaces like my blood is a hundred percent adrenaline.

"Scrap those Clankers!" Hrishi bellows as Keilani passes the ball up the field to me. I laugh as I run. We don't have to guess what he's thinking either. We all speak nerd.

I get two more shots on goal, but their keeper is solid, stuffing it back at me both times. Frustrating, since I'm trying to honor Hrishi's wishes. He sounds like he might have a stroke if I don't.

"Come on." I breathe hard, as I watch our defenders working

their slow way up the field. The Warriors have gotten better. They're making us work this season.

Dad, Budge, and Janie cheer from the sideline. I want to do this for them as much as I want to do it for Hrishi.

As Kaylee brings the ball up the field, setting up a pass to Keilani, Dad stands—his body coiled like he'll spring into the game himself.

I can't help smiling, even as I rock forward on my feet, light and ready.

Dad makes it to most of my games now, and he stands like this whenever watching helpless from a chair gets too intense for him to handle.

Keilani receives the pass. Moves it up the field perfectly. Time's got to be almost up. This is our moment.

She scans the field, eyes bouncing between me and Mackelle for a split second before sending the ball right to me.

Yes!

I trap it perfectly, pull it back from the midfielder barreling straight at me, and spin to head for goal.

But out of nowhere, the Warriors' tiny, sneaky right defender burns straight toward me.

"Nope!" I yell. "My ball." My game, and no one is taking it.

We grapple with our feet, and I'm inching closer to their goal, but it's not enough. The whistle will blow and the game can't end like this. Or worse, with her sending the ball up the line so her team can score on Brianna.

"Morgan," Mackelle calls from right field, where her defender, now rushing me, has left her wide open.

I only pause for a nanosecond before I connect with the ball.

The long pass is solid, clean, and this time, it's Mackelle who's the finisher—sending the ball straight and true into the Warriors' net, as *she* scores one for the Republic, even though she couldn't tell Rex from any other clone if he head-butted her with his custom-painted helmet.

The play took the wind out of me, and I hold still for a second, gasping in air as the whistle blows.

Then I run to join the messy tangle of my team as we jump in a tight huddle and shout our victory cry to the blazing sky.

"You were amazing." Dad and I walk with his arm around my shoulder. Ahead, Hrishi tries to sprint-pull the soccer wagon, full to the giggling, bouncing brim with Budge and Janie.

"Thanks." I'm dripping sweat, still breathing hard. "I didn't score." A tiny part of me wonders if I'd kept the ball, if I could have made it past that scrappy defender and finished the game myself.

"I'm prouder that you didn't."

I look up, and from the Way-To-Go-Morgan smile beaming off his face, it's like he knows how hard it was to send the glory Mackelle's way. She, Keilani, and I might spend lots of time running soccer plays, and we might sit together at lunch most days. But Mackelle is still pretty sure of everything, still pretty squealy about boys, and still . . . well, I'm not gonna lie. Sometimes I still wish it was just me, Keilani, and Hrishi.

But you can't just wish away the things that are hard.

I could say all this to Dad, but I'm pretty sure he already gets it. We've gone through a lot of lemon drops lately.

He helped me figure out what to say when I apologized to Keilani about Brownie Night. And he was right about the part that she would forgive me.

He wasn't kidding about being a boy expert either. His two-part advice about fixing things with Hrishi has worked just fine so far.

1. Kick his toes like always.
2. Remember to be Normal Morgan instead of the Mackelle-Morgan hybrid I became for one awful day back in May.
3. Tell Hrishi my Galactic Graffiti was just to finish his third-grade dare so he'd finally stop bugging me about it, period.
4. Wait and see.

That's four parts. But whatever. I'm not perfect at lists either.

"Hey, Morgan!" Keilani races across the field toward me, still red-cheeked and shiny from our win.

When she gets to me, she pauses, shifts, and looks down at her cleats.

We're a work in progress too. Where we used to say everything, now we say most things.

"Yeah?"

"We were thinking"— she gestures at Mackelle and Brianna and Tasha, hanging back with their families. "Remember what we did after last time we played the Warriors?"

My chest tightens, and I feel the button, trying to close me up for the first time in a couple of weeks.

"Yeah." It comes out as a whisper.

"Some of the girls from the team were thinking we could all go celebrate with some karaoke and Indian food. Like . . . Mama Bell did with us."

I suck in a breath. "Mama Bell" is one of the things we don't say very often.

"It's okay if that's a bad idea."

"No." I spread a smile over my face, and try to let myself enjoy life. It gets easier with practice. "It's a great idea."

Keilani's real smile comes back out then.

"Dad?"

He pauses. I can see how badly he wants to take us, but he's working on another deadline, and taking time away for my game today was tricky enough.

I should just go back with them. Help Janie make dinner—it's her night, and I already talked her out of homemade pizza, and into simpler, tidier mac and cheese.

Think your way around it. Almost-Mom's words find me for the first time in a few weeks.

I smile. "Or maybe," I suggest, "I could go with Keilani, and they could drop me back home after. So you could get your work done?"

"Nice," says Hrishi drily as he drags the wagon back around and offers the handle to Dad. "It's my restaurant, and I'm not even invited."

"Goober," Keilani says. "Of course you're invited."

"Yeah." I elbow him. "How else am I getting free dessert?"

"Hmph." Hrishi folds his arms. "Who says you will?"

I ignore him. "Please, Dad?"

"Yes! Please?" Janie begs. "If Morgan goes, I can make whatever I want for dinner!"

"Puleeease, don't let her make chili volcanoes!" Budge moans. "They are DEE SGUS DING!"

Dad shakes his head, overpowered by all three of us at once. But he hands me cash from his wallet. "Have fun. Call if you need a ride home. It's a school night. By eight-thirty I'd better see you in your PJs, brushing your teeth."

"Thanks. I will." To reassure him, I hold up the new phone I earned with chores and babysitting after drowning Mom's in Sulphur Creek.

Keilani pulls me to a run, as we cross the field to join our friends. And as we pile into the cars and head off for Patel's, I'm almost all the way happy.

Almost—because of nagging little things.

Like how instead of telling me everything, now there are some things Keilani talks with Mackelle about, and others she talks with me about. Some things we all do together, and others—like their mall hangouts—where I opt out. I'm *mostly okay* with these changes, but I'm not gonna lie—I'm hoping things hold steady for a while.

Like how I still don't know if Hrishi has or had an actual crush on me, or if that was just something Mackelle invented to torture everyone. (Foot-kicking and wait-and-seeing isn't the most effective for communicating our deepest thoughts.) It's probably for the best, since I still don't know if I've ever had a crush, what crushes feel like, or why anyone would want one when they only seem to mess things up.

Still, I'm almost all the way happy.

Almost—because of the biggest thing too.

Because I still can't imagine a time when heading off to Patel's after a soccer game for a tradition Mom started—without her—won't hurt a bit, like so many things still do.

Then again, two months ago I couldn't imagine that Dad and I would be launched successfully out of Plan B, and living our New Plan A.

Which we definitely are. *Almost* all of the time.

And who knows what could happen? Like Mom said: *Your New Plan A will hold possibilities you may never have imagined.*

So for now I'm okay if we wait and see.

Author's Note

THE STORY OF
THE LEMON DROPS

The tradition of Lemon Drops began in our home after I nearly died of a pulmonary embolism, and my then eleven-year-old daughter visited the school psychologist for help with the resulting anxiety. The counselor gave her a lemon drop, encouraging her to notice how the flavor changes—starting with sour, then mellowing to sweet. She pointed out that difficult conversations may also start out sour—complicated, tense, or scary. But when we share our truest thoughts and feelings with someone we trust, the sweet quickly follows.

For years now, whenever one of my children needs all of my focus for an emotionally fraught conversation, they ask me for a Lemon Drop—which for us means the talk, not the candy that inspired the tradition. As much as I love my kids, I'm also busy, often distracted. But when someone requests a Lemon Drop, we immediately put aside distractions, go alone to my room, and focus on heart-to-heart communication. The results have been beautiful, often sparing us from later stress and heartache because we've established a safe space for sharing vital thoughts, feelings, and life events. For more information about difficult conversations, or about starting your own Lemon Drop tradition, visit www.HeatherClarkBooks.com.

About the Author

Heather Clark grew up near the Rocky Mountains of Canada, then followed the mountain range south to her current home in Utah, where she lives with her husband and three children who inspire the books she writes. Heather's work as a writer, photographer, and teacher helps her see the beauty and unique value in every person. After dealing with her own childhood anxiety and OCD, Heather is passionate about representing neurodiverse children powerfully in fiction. When she's not working, you can find Heather camping, hiking, boardgaming, or reading and celebrating books at MGBookParty.com. You can learn more about Heather and her books at HeatherClarkBooks.com. *Lemon Drop Falls* is her debut novel.

Acknowledgments

It takes a village to grow a novel, and a thriving metropolis to raise an author. I can't sufficiently thank everyone who has mentored, nurtured, and empowered me on this path to publication, but this is the part where I try.

Thank you to:

My dream agent, Sarah Davies—the one that got away, until we found each other again.

Thank you for wisdom, honesty, kindness, and faith. I'll never forget that first call when I knew with every word that it didn't matter who else offered. Also for building the Greenhouse Literary community—a source of delightful friendships and support.

Mari Kesselring for loving Morgan's story enough to champion it so passionately, for expert edits helping it shine, and for showing me over and over why Jolly Fish was the right home for my debut. Also Emily Temple, whose awesomeness spoiled me for all future publicists, Jake Slavik, who nearly made me cry with this gorgeous book design, the rest of the Jolly Fish team, and dirclumsy for illustrating a fantastic cover that represents the heart of my book so well.

Caryn Caldwell for endless encouragement and guidance,

especially when this story looked dead in the water, and for being brave enough to tell me which parts to scrap.

Cheryl Caldwell for reaching out in the chaos of Pitch Wars to become one of my dearest friends on earth, and for treating my stories like your own.

Lee Ann Setzer for holding my hand along my baby-steps path back to writing. For every minute spent sitting in my green chair.

Nicole Panteleakos for plucking *Lemon Drop Falls* from oblivion, mentoring me like a Pitch Wars Rock Star, and for the most insightful and terrifying editorial notes ever.

Claire Thompson (Morgan's first fan) for crying over multiple drafts and giving me the strength to continue more than once.

Pitch Wars 2019 for ALL THE SUPPORT.

Deon Leavy for teaching my fifth-grade baby the value of a lemon drop in the aftermath of my own pulmonary embolism. You are a beautiful example of the passionate, dedicated educators who change the world one interaction at a time.

Ladies of Original Critiki: My first writing support and forever friends. Thank you, Sabine Berlin, Juliana Montgomery, Rebecca Butler, Sarah Beard, and especially . . .

Janelle Youngstrom—Energizer Bunny of peppy, tough love. You are the reason I've written on more days than I can count.

Seizure Ninjas, or . . . whatever you call yourselves these days. I love you and your no-punches-pulled critique. I needed you, and this book needed you! Special thanks to Janci Patterson, Megan Grey Walker, James Goldberg, Ruth Owen, Heidi Creer.

Write Club, for support, wise critique, companionship. Becca Birkin, Linda White, Anna Read, Cheryl Caldwell, Lee Ann Setzer, Claire Thompson, Jana King. Love sharing this path with you ladies!

Kaylynn Flanders, Lisa Catmull, Rajani LaRocca, Victoria Piontek, Jennifer A. Nielsen, and Dr. Paul Jenkins for expert marketing advice.

Nikki Trionfo for teaching my characters what goals are. And for loving me out of my comfort zone, always.

Martine Leavitt—mentor, encourager, and friend. Also anti-clenching/breathing coach.

Kathryn Thompson for being my person, and for telling me honestly when the story finally got there.

Mom and Dad for lovingly raising me to believe I could do anything I wanted.

Amy Wilson, Alison Bowers, Elin Young, and Hayley Chewins for early reads.

Cindy Baldwin and Amanda Rawson Hill for telling me the naysayers were nuts, and for helping me avoid publication landmines.

Cody, Ellie, Abby, and David—the inspiration for this book, and my greatest joy. Thank you for all the encouragement, love, and patience with Mom going "blue" to write and edit for hours. Thank you for filling my life with light. I love you all forever.